"Annie (...) my girlfriend." Ash leaned over and gave Annie a kiss on the cheek.

She was dumbfounded, frozen with her mouth open. In fact, she felt like she was going to turn to stone. She assumed Ash was kidding and that he'd admit to the joke in a minute. Instead, he turned his face toward her wide-open eyes. He nodded his chin down and then up, motioning for her to say something, urging her on.

"Yeah," Annie squeaked out, without conviction. He wanted her to pretend to be with him? Pretend to be a couple? If only he knew what torture that would be for her. That it was an unreasonable request.

But there was so much he didn't know.

Ash, she silently pleaded. *Don't make me pretend to love you. Or pretend not to.*

Dear Reader,

I don't know about you but I'm a sucker for a "second-time around" story. Annie and Ash were merely twenty-two-years young when they first spotted each other as beacons in the stormy waters of their destructive upbringings. Because of their previous wounds, they couldn't give themselves to each other then.

What a difference ten years brings! Both still think they'll live lives of solitude and distrust, however, the love gods have a different idea. Add to their tale the romance and majesty of New York. It won't be easy to get inside each other's hearts, but these two can't help it.

I've got a soft spot for their road to reunion because my husband and I are second-timers, too. Apparently we had to be immature, petty and dramatic so we could break up and then finally find our way back to each other. Turns out he was my *meant to be*. Just like Annie and Ash.

I hope you enjoy their story. Thanks for reading.

Andrea x

NEW YORK FLING
WITH THE TYCOON

ANDREA BOLTER

Harlequin
ROMANCE

Harlequin®
ROMANCE

ISBN-13: 978-1-335-47048-5

New York Fling with the Tycoon

Harlequin Enterprises ULC
22 Adelaide St. West, 41st Floor
Toronto, Ontario M5H 4E3, Canada
www.Harlequin.com

Printed in U.S.A.

Recycling programs for this product may not exist in your area.

Andrea Bolter has always been fascinated by matters of the heart. In fact, she's the one her girlfriends turn to for advice with their love lives. A city mouse, she lives in Los Angeles with her husband and daughter. She loves travel, rock 'n' roll, sitting at cafés and watching romantic comedies she's already seen a hundred times. Say hi at andreabolter.com.

Books by Andrea Bolter

Harlequin Romance

Billion-Dollar Matches

Caribbean Nights with the Tycoon

Her Las Vegas Wedding
The Italian's Runaway Princess
The Prince's Cinderella
His Convenient New York Bride
Captivated by Her Parisian Billionaire
Wedding Date with the Billionaire
Adventure with a Secret Prince
Pretend Honeymoon with the Best Man
Jet-Set Escape with Her Billionaire Boss

Visit the Author Profile page at Harlequin.com.

For my TSG Friends

Praise for
Andrea Bolter

"From that first book I was completely hooked
with her stories and this is easily my all-time favorite
to date. I thoroughly enjoyed this, [as] it's the
perfect little escapism."

—*Goodreads* on
Captivated by Her Parisian Billionaire

CHAPTER ONE

ASH MORETTI?

Annie Butterfield had just walked in and kicked off her shoes when the phone rang. Retrieving it from her pocket, she had proceeded barefoot across the wooden floorboards to open the gingerbread windows of her Victorian house and let the natural light of sunset into her living room. But she stopped dead in her tracks, in the middle of the room, when she swiped the screen to the notification that Ash Moretti was calling. The mere sight of his name gave an apprehensive brace to her shoulders.

While they were technically coworkers, he'd never called her at home, although she supposed he wouldn't have the slightest idea of the current whereabouts of her cell phone. Yet somehow his call invaded her personal space.

"This is Annie." He'd called her, so it was a stupid greeting, but she was nervous, and so out it fell.

"How's the Mile High?" he asked in his unmistakable low-pitched voice, making reference to Denver's nickname as the city located a mile above sea level.

Night had probably settled over New York by now, with Ash still working and maybe assuming she was still in her office, the time zone in Denver being two hours earlier. A flutter raced down the skin on her arms at the thought of Ash, with his stare that had always had more power over her than it should. Tall and lean, he had an intensity and tautness in both his face and body that showed he hadn't had an easy life.

"The leaves are turning."

"Pretty."

It wasn't like Ash to chitchat but she guessed he felt he had to make pleasantries before announcing why he was calling. They were colleagues at Edward Jameson Wealth Management, known simply as EJ, a financial planning firm based in New York with satellite offices across the globe. Ash had been born and bred on the East Coast, and stayed on there once he and Annie had both completed Edward Jameson's mentorship program ten years ago. By contrast, Annie had accepted a position in the company's Denver office, her hometown.

She and Ash rarely had occasion to talk one-on-one so it was, in fact, odd that he was calling. And that wasn't the only cause of her trepidation, she thought as she blew air out of her cheeks. What did he want? "Same in the Big App?" Back to the weather.

"Yeah, though it smells like winter."

Winter in New York. Ten years ago. They had both been twenty-two, recent college grads, lucky to have been chosen for the finance industry mentorship and to be ensconced in EJ's gleaming offices on Wall Street where fortunes were made and commissions funded salaries.

The mentorship holiday party. The eggnog was rich and expensive. Her dress wasn't—a plain red that had seen more than one Christmas. But what had been building since the September retreat that had kicked off the program had finally exploded in a dark office cubicle while the party went on in the conference center down the hall. It had been one time. One breathtaking, earth-bending act of lovemaking that informed everything in her life that came after it. An interlude frozen in time. A holiday season Annie had never been able to forget.

"What can I do for you, Ash?" Enough with the awkward opening. She continued in her bare feet to the kitchen, opened one of the beveled wood cabinets to get a glass and poured herself some water which she downed in one sip.

"I need you."

Annie's eyes shut, seemingly of their own volition. *He needed her.* If that wasn't so wrenching, it would be funny. "I doubt it."

Ash Moretti didn't need anyone. Or wouldn't need, anyway.

"It's about Edward's retirement." The great man Edward Jameson was ready to step down and see out the rest of his years at his Long Island mansion with scores of free time to devote to his beloved charities. During his distinguished career, he'd given a lot to his mentees, to his employees, to Wall Street in general. He'd more than earned his time to relax and let others carry on his good name, with Ash taking over as CEO.

"I hear you're planning several events to fete him."

"That's what I'm calling about. I need you to come to New York and run this for me."

"Run what?" She looked down to her feet, spreading her toes open and then closing them together. The sound of Ash's voice had a physical effect on her, made her hyperaware of her body.

"These retirement parties. We hired an outside party coordinator, Marissa, who made a mess of things and I let her go. You're our best events manager. I should have kept it in house all along." The company had four event managers, their territories divided regionally. Annie was in charge of the Western United States and Asia-Pacific. "Everything needs to go right. This is for Edward, after all."

Annie's lips cracked into a small smile although there was no one there to see it. She took pride in her work and appreciated that Ash mentioned it. The pull of her own lips made her think of his, pink and firm and powerful. "So hire another events company. You were right that none of us in house has time for a week's slate of activities."

"I want you." He said those words confidently, aggressively even. She had to fight them off like shards of kryptonite attacking her. *I want you.* What an irony. If he only knew.

To the matter at hand, she'd already heard through the grapevine that Marissa hadn't been doing a good job. And Franco, who oversaw the East Coast and South American territories, was new and couldn't be expected to have a project like this dumped in his lap.

Annie had been in the Denver office all of these ten years since the mentorship program. She'd stayed local so she could be with her mother and brothers after her parents divorced, at least that's what she'd told herself and everyone else for the first few years.

Now she'd grown stagnant.

She and Ash had been on level footing when they'd left the mentorship, but he'd risen to second in command and she'd let herself get stuck in Denver with no room to grow. Still, anything involving working closely with Ash wouldn't be a good idea. She wondered what memories he carried from those younger days.

She poured a second glass of water. He was

making her mouth dry. "What exactly are you asking?"

"I want you to come to New York and take charge of the retirement week. Four events, three weeks from now, one of them a closing night charity gala."

"Three weeks! What about my responsibilities here? I've got a four-day convention in Osaka to put together."

"We'd have to pass on some extra work to Majid in Dubai. He'll handle it. You supervise this. In fact, we're considering some restructuring anyway after we give Edward a proper send-off."

Restructuring? That was a lot of information coming at her all at once.

"Why don't I help out as I can remotely? I can do a lot from here." She certainly didn't fly to Vancouver or Seoul for every single event she oversaw.

"I need you. In person." Again, little words but strung together hit her with meanings beyond what had been intended. Which was why collaborating with Ash on any level was a very bad idea. For most of these past ten years they'd not had much overlap, seeing each other in person at all-company meetings or special occasions, and usually in groups big enough that she could keep her distance from him.

Although she hadn't failed to notice the way he sometimes set his gaze right on her during video conferences, piercing into her eyes or letting his glance dip to her collarbones or even lower, making the most businesslike conversation have a secret content she pretended to ignore. Those big deep brown eyes of his, focused right into her, as if they were entitled to, altogether wicked. And possessive. No, she could not go to New York and work side by side with Ash Moretti.

It should have been okay. They'd cleared the air ten years ago, deciding that neither of them could pursue anything further than a few months of flirtation culminating in one mistletoe-fueled blaze, followed by a spring of smoldering embers that they'd deliberately kept from reigniting. Yet it didn't feel okay. Annie sighed. What was she going to do, say no to Ash asking her to help when he really needed her for Edward's sake? Plus, as incoming CEO he was theoretically her boss now if he pressed it. "What is the situation?"

"The nightmare you'd expect. Staff at the

venues and party vendors not given proper directions, food and decor not settled. Invitations went out months ago so we have scores of RSVPs."

"How did it get that bad?"

"I've got a million things going on taking over as CEO. I thought I could trust Marissa to do her damn job. Which she assured me she was doing. Until I received a couple of concerned calls and I checked into it."

"Oh, heavens. How could she have screwed up so badly?" Annie could hear the stress in Ash's voice. It wasn't just a point of pride to her that when she ran an event she did everything within her control to do it to perfection. It was simply how she worked. And Ash had a similar expectation of himself in all of his endeavors, as she had witnessed from the beginning. "So you have access to all the files regarding every aspect of the events and you can easily turn it over to someone else?"

"I hope so."

"Can you give me the log-ons and I'll see what I can find?"

"There are a lot of specifics printed out, signed contracts, people to meet with, design details and seating plans. The events are very unique. Annie, please come to New York and help me out. Is there something keeping you from saying yes?"

If she looked under those words she could feel insulted. He knew that she was unmarried and childless in Denver, everyone in the company knew those basic things about each other. Thankfully, he wouldn't know about Jack. She was happy no one at EJ knew about that disaster, glad she'd never invited her ex to anything work related.

Was Ash implying that she had nothing better to do? And did that maybe ring true? She was on autopilot, not excited by anything anymore. "I do want to see that everything is right for Edward." Who'd given both of them so much.

She knew she needed change. She wasn't miserable, but she was certainly itchy to not be at the end of her road. Wasn't there something more, a way to grow, to further herself both privately and professionally?

"As I mentioned, we're planning some re-evaluating we haven't yet had time for. Edward isn't leaving the company, he just won't be running the day-to-day anymore. He's committing to more and more philanthropy and as an educator for the industry. We'll have more events and scheduling than ever before. I haven't announced anything but I can see a leadership vice president role emerging in overseeing all of that. Is that something you'd consider? If you still don't like New York we could consider headquartering the position in Dubai."

Don't like New York? Of course she liked New York, its beats and excitement. He didn't know that it wasn't the city she had to get away from when she returned to Denver after the mentorship.

"It would be great for my execs and board to have a chance to see you work in person on these events and know what a perfect choice you'd be."

Annie's kitchen suddenly seemed to be devoid of oxygen as she found it necessary to sit down on one her stools at the kitchen counter beside where she had been standing for the entire conversation. Was Ash seriously saying that he had her in mind for a promotion that could radically change her life? Him, of all people?

She looked around the kitchen of her lovely Victorian-style home. She'd saved money for the down payment and become the sole owner. She had friends. Her current position gave her travel. It wasn't like she could find fault with her current life. Yet she yearned for more. Something more.

"A VP position?"

"I'd like to talk more with you about it."

Ash was calling her. The something more that never was. Which had been at least fifty percent her doing. The last time they had both been on a teleconference call a couple of months ago, he'd stood leaning back against a meeting room wall, his eyes fixed on her, almost communicating something to her that was ticking in his head, his glare transmitting across the miles. Was he creating that VP position with her in mind? Did he think they could work together with the past being of no relevance? Was she just an employee on a flowchart that he'd thought of a better way to utilize? And now with his need for help on the Edward farewell, he was dangling it in front of her earlier than he had intended to?

She could imagine him in his custom-made, impeccably tailored brown suit. Crisp white shirt and green tie, brown hair that almost grazed his shoulders. As much as he presented himself as a Wall Street professional, she'd always seen that he was different. A little off. A little hardened. She wondered if anyone who worked at EJ knew how hard his road to here had been. Whether anyone had seen the tattoos on his chest that she had when she first met him at the mentor retreat.

She hadn't seen those tattoos long enough to commit them to memory even though she'd thought about them ever since. They weren't the sort of inking that was carefully and intricately designed and presketched by a fine artist who rendered true art onto people's skin. No, Ash's tattoos were sloppy, single-colored, letters and symbols and drawings here and there on his body. They were ugly. And there were several of them, too many. They all looked like they were done by amateurs without proper equipment on drunken nights, and maybe even regretted.

For all Annie knew, now ten years down the line, he may have had them removed. It was ridiculous that she was even thinking about them now.

"Will you come?"

She still thought about him every day of her life. Could she take a chance and spend time with him again, working closely together, knowing they were long past the possibility of anything personal between them moving forward from an ancient holiday party he probably didn't even remember?

Because maybe he'd never given a second thought to what had, and hadn't, happened back then. Like her, at twenty-two, he'd been already sure that he was never going to get married or even be in a serious relationship. Not after the things they'd each been through. And unless she'd missed some office scuttlebutt, he never had. She'd always figured it had to do with his father, who he'd talked about in only the bitterest of tones, suggesting a damaged childhood. Like hers. They had been kindred spirits that way from the beginning. She wondered if he'd ever reflected back on the time they'd spent together. And what he saw.

Could doing this make her past with Ash finally become water under the bridge for her? Facing him head-on as a catharsis—maybe it would be a release. To be free from the chains of her feelings for him she'd been bound by for all of this time. She'd devoted so much thought and longing to him, for what she claimed her rational self didn't even want.

Plus, there was Edward to consider. Edward, who had tragically lost his wife to illness after finally finding love late in life. Even if Annie hadn't progressed as far in the company as Ash had, it was not of Edward's doing. She only had herself to blame. She'd held herself back. Her mentor had shown her nothing but opportunity and kindness. Shouldn't she lend her considerable skills where they were needed most, for his benefit?

She adjusted the headband that perpetually held her hair away from her face. "Tomorrow is Thursday," she said, finally reasoning out a plan. "Why don't I get on a plane and come to New York for a long weekend and we'll see after that?" It was a weekend. She wasn't making any promises.

"You're a lifesaver. I'll arrange everything. You won't regret it."

Her heartbeat fluttered. She wasn't as sure about that as he was.

"Ash, Zara Parker is here," Ash's PA Irene's voice came through the speaker on Ash Moretti's desk phone. She only interrupted him in that manner if she needed to.

He grimaced. Ugh, not Zara again. Edward's stepdaughter, who held no position in the company, found her way into the offices more days than not. Of course, security guards and assistants in the executive offices weren't going to deny her entry. She was family, or sort of, a spoiled society girl in her early twenties with no apparent occupation. Who'd seemed to have gotten over her mother's sad death rather quickly.

Ash pushed his leather chair back from his desk to stand. There was nothing to do with Zara other than work around her demands of the day. He regarded her as an occupational hazard he just had to put up with at this point. Soon enough, Edward wouldn't be coming into the office every day and Zara would be easier to turn away. "Go ahead and send her in."

"Will do."

The double doors to his office cracked open. If he had his eyes closed, he'd still know Zara had arrived. He wondered exactly how much perfume her stepfather, Edward, had to pay for to create such a waft of cloying florals. There was also the identifiable clang of the excessive amount of jewelry she always wore, as well.

She made a dramatic gesture of pushing the double doors open as wide as she could, stepping in and then turning to close them as if she was about to let Ash in on a national secret.

"What can I do for you today?" If his tone was exhausted, it was legitimate. Nuisance didn't even begin to describe her frequent visits.

Wearing a tight dress in a pink that looked like stomach medicine but he believed was called fuchsia, wobbling in on a pair of high-heeled sandals she exclaimed, "I brought you lunch, silly. Remember I told you yesterday that I was going to?" She held up a sort of designer picnic basket—white leather criss-crosses standing in for the straw weave, which he was sure cost four figures.

"And don't you remember, Zara, how I told you yesterday, as I have many times before that, you can't simply barge into my office anytime you feel like it?" Which was, of course, a lie because she both could and did.

"I know A-ash," she somehow stretched his

name into two syllables. "It'll be so much easier when we stop hiding our relationship."

"We don't have a relationship, Zara."

"Not yet," she answered with an exaggerated and lascivious wink that was so ridiculous he almost laughed. This had been going on since she'd met him at a company party where she hadn't belonged. She seemed to think that if she was persistent enough, he'd agree to *be* with her. That was never going to happen. Nonetheless, he put up with her because he felt compelled to keep Edward and the rest of the company from knowing about her antics. It would cause Edward stress, embarrassment and possibly pain, as Zara's mother, the wife and love Edward hadn't found until he was an older man, had taken ill and died only six months earlier. It wouldn't do for the office to know how inappropriate Zara was.

He had to get this indiscreet little mess off his hands. He thought of Annie, who after their conversation last night was winging her way to New York at this very moment. Maybe Annie could solve his problem. Perhaps with them working together on the retirement events, she could be a buffer that would keep Zara away from him at least until the event week was over.

Annie Butterfield was on her way to New York. His tongue swept across his upper teeth.

Ignoring Zara, he tapped into his computer for a flight tracker to see exactly where her plane was at this moment, his own impulse surprising him. He pressed the intercom button. "Irene, could you see Miss Jameson out?"

"What?" Zara gave him a pouty look but cooperated when Irene opened the door.

"I have work I have to do."

"Oh, okay I guess. I'll see you later, Ash." It sounded like a plea.

After she swished away he instructed, "Irene, I'm going to have lunch with Edward at my apartment. Order food and have the driver who's picking up Annie Butterfield take her straight there from the airport."

"Certainly."

After his driver dropped him off at the entrance to the building he lived in, Ash rode the elevator straight up to his penthouse, watching out the glass windows as he shot seemingly into the ether, so high that he was secluded from life on earth, which was how he liked it. He stepped into the foyer, the grandeur of the Carrara marble floor juxtaposed with a couple of pieces of abstract art on the walls; all of it very private, very his, a fortress holding as many secrets as he wanted it to. He removed his jacket, hooked it on a coatrack and took off his tie. He picked up the lunch that had already been delivered and left on the entry table.

Edward was expected within minutes and it'd only be a couple of hours until Annie's arrival. Everything was as he preferred it in the huge great room, no clutter whatsoever, just views, views and more views, his penthouse looking out over Lower Manhattan, the Wall Street skyscrapers where his orbit was located. His home was on the thirty-ninth floor and the EJ office a dozen blocks south on the forty-fifth. Ash both lived and worked in the sky.

No sooner had he checked his phone for updates than a lobby doorman informed him that Edward was there. Ash opened the door and greeted his boss, mentor and friend. "Come in, I've just gotten home myself." He wasn't going to mention that Edward's stepdaughter had been the reason he'd fallen a bit behind schedule today. He'd never discussed

Zara with Edward, and hoped never to at that. The older man didn't need the extra burden of a wild stepdaughter.

"You must be swamped," Edward said upon entry. The two men embraced, something Edward had only recently instigated, perhaps in acknowledgement that they wouldn't be seeing each other every day anymore as they had for years. Ash went along with the gesture that fit in with the sometimes-paternal feelings Edward showed for him, the counterpoint to the father who had frequently reduced Ash to nothing.

Ash counted his blessings that Edward had changed his luck. Or perhaps he had changed his own luck, and Edward had magically been there with the pathway out. In any case, what he owed the man was immeasurable. He had a moment's sigh of relief that Annie was on her way and would surely help the retirement send-off be a grand and fitting tribute.

He'd seen performance reviews over the years and been to many events Annie had helmed and he knew her work was superb. He was quite sure that after the retirement ruckus quieted down he'd want to promote her to the VP position he intended to create. He'd occasionally reflected on the kismet they'd felt at twenty-two. They'd been clear then, just as he still was, that a romantic relationship was not in the cards. So, nothing between them had gone further than a single encounter. It was what they'd agreed on. Not that he hadn't wondered what if…

But those were the kind of thoughts he knew to shoo away. They could both benefit from Annie's professionalism to help the company continue to prosper and expand.

Ash grabbed the food and they sat down at what Ash referred to as the breakfast nook, an alcove painted bright white with colorful paintings of fruits and vegetables on the wall. It had a built-in semicircular booth upholstered with comfy orange cushions. He laid out the lunch. "I'll slog through it. I finally finished the Adams and Adams recommendations. By the way, you're looking well." Edward's thick white hair offset the tan acquired from time at the seashore. He'd had such a gray pallor in the months since Betty's death, Ash was glad to see him finally more animated.

Edward glanced around the space, not having been over in a while. "I'm so glad you bought this place, Ash," he said, referring to the time five years ago when Ash had had an especially good year in commissions, real estate prices had been favorable and Edward had counseled him to buy a property. "It'll be a good place to start a family. Then you'll probably move out to Long Island for the land."

"There you go again," Ash teased.

"I've told you before, I'd have given anything to have found the love of my life sooner and to have held on to her longer." Sadly only a few years into Edward's marital bliss, Betty had been diagnosed with a late-stage cancer and had been gone within months. "All the success in the world still isn't enough to make life complete."

"That's not for me." The words didn't trip out easy no matter how many times he'd uttered them. Edward knew something about Ash's childhood, about the unloving father who'd taken his unhappiness out on his only child. Edward didn't have the whole story but he knew that Ash had decided to go it in this world alone.

Ash had stuck to his credo throughout his twenties, with only casual affairs that had never gone further. But lately, with Edward's retirement and Ash's promotion to CEO, all of those considerations had been popping up. About what mattered. What defined success.

For some unexplainable reason he thought of Annie again, whose flight would be in its final hour toward New York. He thought about that ridiculous interaction with Zara, and how different Annie was with her soft voice. In her plain business clothes and little in the way of *va va boom*, Annie actually had a quiet beauty that was very earthen and true.

Which was neither here nor there, merely an observation.

They dug into their Cobb salads. Atop crisp lettuce sat chunks of roasted chicken breast in rows alongside appetizing fresh chopped tomato, crumbled blue cheese, broken pieces of thick bacon, quartered hard-boiled eggs, sliced ripe avocado and diced chives, along with two choices of dressings. On the side were warm rye rolls and pots of soft butter.

"With you taking over the helm," Edward persisted, "I know our board and clients would like to see you settled down, having some kids."

"Is this why you wanted to meet with me

today? For *this* conversation again? Or did you have something actually pressing?"

Edward laughed warmly. "No. Although it's as good a reason as any. Mark my words. When you share your life, you don't get half, you get double."

"So, to what do I owe the honor?" Ash broke open a warm roll and used the knife provided to smear some butter on it.

"I think there's some sensitivity about the Burrell Enterprises account I want to be sure is resolved before I hand it over to you." As Edward explained his concerns, Ash checked the flight tracker on his phone again and had a moment of flashback to the smart girl from Denver with whom he'd shared a time long ago that he'd never forgotten.

CHAPTER TWO

"GLAD YOU COULD make this work." Edward had already left by the time the doorman let Ash know that Annie had arrived and was on her way up. Until the moment he opened the penthouse door to greet her, Ash hadn't seen her in person since the summer conference, and here it was autumn. He hadn't even spoken with her much lately as their agendas didn't overlap, other than attendance during teleconferences. "It's nice to see you in person again. If I hadn't told you before, that was a tremendous conference in San Diego you put together."

"Thank you, Ash." Her voice was even more buttery than he'd recalled. She stepped into his apartment and he had the strangest feeling of intimacy at her entry, something he'd never felt before. His apartment was massive for just one person. He was an absolute cliché of the wealthy bachelor who, after working in his office on The Street traveled just a little bit uptown to roam around in his castle in the clouds, often paying little mind to his surroundings. "Oh my, this is massive."

"I know. Edward counseled me on buying it for a great price during a market downturn. Let me show you around."

"Okay." She left her wheeled suitcase at the door and looked around at where to put her purse. He pointed to a table at the entry, where he always put his own wallet and keys. That was strangely homey, too, watching her putting her things down alongside his. It touched his heart, rather than put him off as it usually did when he saw other people doing cutesy things like that.

The afternoon light through his wall of windows caught flickers of Annie's blond hair. She wasn't much more than five feet tall with pale skin and luminescent green eyes. She wore a white blouse tucked into black trousers and a black headband. For the first time it occurred to him that it was a strange choice to have the airport driver bring her here, instead of to the office or to a hotel. Hotel. Oops, he hadn't even remembered to book her a hotel.

His place was huge, she could just stay here. They'd never know the other was there.

Annie and he had developed a certain closeness during that mentorship program, as people do when they're forced to spend a lot of concentrated time together. Even before they'd taken things further that one night, they'd actually found a certain comradery in how guarded they both were, and over the fall that had been the opening quarter of the one-year program, had confided a little on why. They'd had a couple of honest talks that were still the most Ash had ever opened up to anyone. He'd never forgotten that. In spite of all of that, or maybe because of it, they'd kept a distance for the past ten years, safely secured at separate locations of the EJ company.

He thought about Edward needling him again about a stable lifestyle, one that clients would especially like to see now that Ash was at the helm. Hmm, he saw a flash of what it would be like to be with Annie, seeing her put her purse down in the entryway every evening, and doing all the normal things people did together every day. He subtly shook his head to himself, a reminder to stick to the here and now.

"Obviously, this is the great room." He continued with his penthouse tour, walking her across the central area, the crossroads of the apartment. A sitting area held two large sofas facing each other, done in a fabric of pale yellow. A glass coffee table stood in between them, and white leather armchairs added to the conversation area. "My living room, for entertaining, which I do none of." He said it with a smile. For some reason he felt like laughing at himself.

With another sweep of his hand he brought her attention to the entertainment center on the other side of the room. An enormous screen hung in front of two rows of chairs, made to look like a mini movie theater or sports stadium. Each seat had a little lap table with a cup holder for drinks and room for snacks. Perfect for a watch party or something like that, though he mainly watched on his own.

"That's very cool."

He liked that she liked it. "My dining room table. Oak and steel. Seats twelve. All picked out by a decorator, of course. Amount of dinner parties I've had here? Zero."

"You like living in a place you don't make use of?"

He was surprised, but not displeased, by her challenge. Sure, he didn't take full advantage of the apartment like a family might, but this penthouse was important to him because he'd worked hard for it. There was the taste of revenge in it, gaining victory over the early years that had tried to keep him from every bit of pride or joy possible.

He'd decided early on after the horrors of his family that he was never going to marry or have kids, so it had been easy to keep his eye on financial success. The apartment was a trophy. It didn't make up for the suffering the past had scarred him with. But he enjoyed the comfort; he wouldn't deny it.

"Where do you live? In Denver proper?"

"Yeah, Capitol Hill. I own a little Victorian."

"Good for you. I'm glad you were able to buy a home."

He remembered that she'd had family strife, as well. That they both vowed to become professionals and to be alone. Not to ever let a relationship hurt them again. "Still sticking to your rule of no close relationships?"

"No risk of hurt that way. You?"

"One little mistake, otherwise yes." Why

in ten years of seeing each other a couple of times a year hadn't they caught up? For him it had been because she was dangerous. She knew him, a little anyway, on the inside, and he didn't want to dredge the past back up. Better to keep it buried, to keep his distance. Which was easy when there were always clusters of coworkers between them.

"Glad to hear. Not glad to hear you aren't in a relationship, exactly, uh, but I mean... That's what you want right? Like me." He was fumbling all over himself. It was quite something to be face-to-face with Annie again without other people around. He hadn't given thought to how that might feel. He supposed that was the modern world now—once you interacted with someone mostly on telescreens, you tended to forget that people gave off a tangible aura, an essence not gleaned from the screen. Her presence charged him up a little, made him a little more alive.

"Like you."

He went on with his tour, pointing to his master suite, not intending to bring her in as that would seem inappropriate.

"I didn't ask you, what hotel did you book me at?"

"I haven't."

"You haven't?" A look of confusion came over her lovely face and he was sorry to have caused that.

"Let's get that taken care of. Although, you're welcome to stay here. I have plenty of room for guests." He pointed the opposite direction of his master suite.

"I don't think that would be app…"

"Let me show you," he interrupted. "It's about two blocks from here, thatta way." His attempt at another joke about the apartment was met with a quizzical look.

"Okay."

He led her down the hallway on the other side of the great room. "Here's my home office. I've got a setup for three people to be working here with all the latest tech. This bedroom has been converted to a personal gym. Here's another sitting area with sofas and a TV screen mounted on the wall."

"Nice library." She pointed to the stocked bookshelves.

One sunny room had been done in soft colors and gauzy curtains. "This is meant as a meditation room, a getaway within my getaway. I keep meaning to use it."

"Uh-huh."

There were three guest bedrooms. Ash chose the biggest one, which had a lavishly appointed en suite bathroom. "Why don't you take this one?" The room was furnished in white with sage green accents. A king-size bed was held by a light wood frame. There were two armchairs with a table between them and another sweeping view of the city. A refreshment counter offered a basket of snacks, another of fruit, a small coffee maker and bottled waters.

"You running your own hotel here, Ash?" Annie smiled.

"As a matter of fact—" he pointed to a closed door with a knob and locks "—you'd be my first guest. There's a separate entrance to this part of the apartment. So if you need to escape from me in the middle of the night, you can." Did he just flirt with her? That was so unlike him.

She raised her eyebrows, yet in a teasing way. "Noted."

"Of course, I barely enter this part of the penthouse. Why don't you stay? It should get some use. It'll be like old times, we can make s'mores out by the fire pit."

"We were in a professional mentorship program together, not middle grade adventure camp. There were no s'mores."

What he'd been referring to was the closeness that he had for a moment with her, the conversations they'd shared—including the most intimate conversation he ever had with anyone. Maybe spending time with Annie again would help confirm whether the vows of solitude he made as a young man were still valid. He hadn't planned any of that when he summonsed her to New York to fix the parties, but suddenly it all made sense. She represented what might have been. If his life had gone in a different direction. "I do have a fabulous fire pit." He gestured to one of the patios outside, accessible through sliding glass doors.

"All the amenities. I bet the guides would give your place five stars."

Jovial banter aside, he needed Annie's help. "My apologies for not thinking to have my assistant book you a hotel." Where had his brain gone? With all the parties in various states of disarray, the firing of the incompetent outside event planner, plus Zara's constant ploy for attention, it slipped his mind. That wasn't like him. "Are you comfortable spending the night and we'll figure it out in the morning?"

Annie hoped that by asking Ash for a few minutes to freshen up, a little bit of time before they launched into the purpose of her visit, which she still knew little about, she wasn't de facto agreeing to stay in his apartment. When they'd talked on the phone yesterday, he said he'd take care of everything regarding her visit. It never occurred to her that he wouldn't have booked her a hotel. Of course the irony was that she was more than capable of taking care of things like arranging travel. "Why don't I just change my clothes, check my messages and I'll be out in a little while?"

"Sure," Ash answered her request.

"Are we going into the EJ office?"

"Not today. We'll set up our situation room in my home office, so we don't have to be concerned about tidying our work up at the end of the day."

She could easily find a hotel if she chose to. But something told her to just stay the night and see how it went. Maybe because she did want to be under his roof. As if her longstanding dreams were leaking into real life.

Um, no, Annie. That was never going to happen.

Ash retrieved her suitcase from the front door foyer and wheeled it in. The sight of him tugging her suitcase, holding something of hers, produced a strange sensation in her, the same one she'd felt when she'd first heard his voice on her cell phone yesterday. Her shoulders arched in a move that was defensive, some kind of alarm alerting her of peril. Maybe it was because, even though she'd seen his handsome, rugged face plenty of times, seen those big hands pick up a pen or crack open a bottle of water, it had been a long time since there had been no buffer of other people to keep her at a distance.

Now in his ginormous penthouse, the vibrations coming off his firm body as he brought her suitcase to her were palpable. He was wearing suit pants and a white shirt with the top button undone, the sleeves cuffed over revealing his slim, muscular, veiny arms. She remembered ten years ago seeing those veins in his arms had fascinated her. The channels in which hot red blood coursed through him was very seductive to a young woman who hadn't felt the arms of men around her. Yes, she'd looked for those veins over the years, on the occasions when his sleeves were rolled up or he wore a T-shirt at company picnics or sports games. Just as she'd wondered about the tattoos on his chest.

He placed her suitcase on a bench that appeared meant for the task. "Come on out when you're ready—I'll be in the office."

"Okay."

He turned to walk away and the sight of his six-foot-plus frame made her cheeks fill with air. She squeaked out a small sound which caused him to turn around. "Is everything okay?"

"Oh, sure, yes, I think my throat is a bit dry." She glanced to the drinks on the counter so that he didn't have to show her what she'd already noticed. Under the same roof, alone, with Ash Moretti was already a lot. One thing she felt certain of was that he was not a monster who would wield his might and authority to coerce a woman into doing something she didn't want to do. She'd be safe spending the night in his mansion that reached the moon.

She'd often wondered if he'd thought about

her in the ten years that had passed with him in New York and her out West. About their connection. By the time the mentorship had been over and jobs were being awarded, their interlude had been destined to become just a memory, a souvenir of that time.

Except that none of that had held true for her. She thought about him day and night, on special occasions and ordinary ones, when she felt elated and when darkness fell on her. He lived inside her soul.

"I'll see you in a few." He turned back to be sure she didn't need anything and then continued toward the office. She instantly noticed that she liked the sight of him walking toward her quite a bit more than him walking away.

Once out of her sight line, she literally used a hand to fan her face like a description of someone about to faint in a historical novel. Her cheeks were so hot that she rushed over to the sink and splashed herself with cold water, turning the heavy nickel faucet handles on and then off. She blotted her face with the plushest cream-colored towel she'd ever used.

Checking herself in the mirror, she saw her skin was flushed. One minute she was at home in Denver kicking off her shoes and in

the next she was in New York at Ash's palace
in the sky! Ash Moretti, who'd occupied so
much space in her heart and mind for so long
that if he knew about it, he'd have to admit
he wasn't playing fair. In fact, he was part of
her DNA. In a way, perhaps, the place he'd secretly taken in her life had crowded out other
possibilities.

Regardless of her shock at being called to
EJ Headquarters like this, it would soon be
time to get to the task at hand. Event planning
was very absorbing with all of its details, and
that would take her mind off being this close
to Ash. At least she hoped it would.

Opening her suitcase, she knew she wanted
to get out of the clothes she'd traveled in, but
she wasn't sure what to wear. Would they
be going out to dinner later, or would it be
a work-through, hovered over laptops and
mindlessly satiating hunger with sustenance
and nothing more? Truth be told, she always
felt self-conscious in big cities like New York
where people dressed so stylishly and cared so
much about their appearance. Fashion wasn't
exactly part of Annie's life, growing up in a
house of discord that had bigger issues than
the possibility of wearing the wrong jacket

with the wrong skirt. Even more ludicrous was that what was really on her mind was what Ash's reaction would be to whatever she reappeared in, as if he would even notice what she was wearing or have any reaction at all.

But when she picked up a peach-colored jersey track suit she brought for lounging around and held it up to herself in the full-length mirror, she quickly deemed that too casual and dropped it back into her suitcase. Flipping through what she'd brought for what was to be only a long weekend, she settled on a pair of dark pants and a black T-shirt. Dull. Like the rest of her wardrobe. She thought about her one boyfriend, Jack, who would criticize her for looking too business-y whatever the occasion.

She'd followed Ash's doings when he was photographed by the media, out on the town with glamazon women. And why wouldn't he be? He was rich, accomplished, and determined to be unattached so there was always someone new on his arm. Annie opened a juice, sipped it. Fashionable, she wasn't. But did one have to be to merely be a coworker of Ash's? She readjusted her usual headband that kept her hair out of her eyes.

"I'm in here." She heard his voice call out once she stepped into the hallway. How did he know she was approaching? Had he heard her open the guest room door? "In the office."

As she approached she saw him sitting at his desk facing the door, his back to the New York skyline that seemed to grace every room on the east side of the penthouse. Ash sat tall and squared into his chair, a sight to behold. He emanated a slow and competent power. It made sense that he rose within the company and would now take the reins. As if he was destined to it. She remembered him telling her once that revenge was a mighty motivator, obviously referring to his family and the problems he had to put aside to ascend. "Hi."

"Why don't you take this one in front of me—" he gestured to the desk that faced him, and the view "—and I'll set up the monitors so we can share files and whatnot." Naturally, he had it all figured out.

"Okay." She took a seat in the sumptuous leather chair provided and tapped open the screen in front of her.

"We've got four events planned."

"What are they?" She opened a new file on the laptop for her own notes. Ash had said he would forward her everything Marissa had worked on, too.

"First we're going to do a company-wide breakfast."

"I did actually get a Save the Date email."

"Thank goodness. We'll do a breakfast here in New York and we'll get online with all of the employees at all of the offices around the world. Tricky with the time zones but everyone has agreed to come at ridiculous hours to get into the spirit of it."

"I love it. I bet I can get food services from all over the globe to deliver American breakfasts so that everyone can be eating the same thing. And I'll make sure all the offices have enough big screens and tech so we can really see each other."

She thought of times with group teleconferences where she had to admit she scanned the screen to try to find Ash in attendance. Just to survey him, to see whether he looked well or drawn. And yes, to think back on his urgent kisses when they were twenty-two, of his hands on her skin, to hear his voice when he spoke. She'd never imagined being in his apartment at thirty-two.

"Once you look over everything, we'll see what needs to be done and we'll task it out."

"That's really a lovely idea, a breakfast where we can all be with Edward together, at least digitally. Did Marissa think of that?"

He raised his eyebrows and tilted his head to the side to shoot her a *you must be kidding* look. "No. She barely understood that technology would allow that. It was actually Edward's idea. I think we started with dinner but then breakfast sounded more novel."

"Okay, what's next?"

"The next event is for the board, stockholders, investors and platinum clients. We're taking over a Broadway theater for a private invitation-only performance of *We Found Home*."

"The Tony-winning musical."

"It's on a Monday when the theaters are dark and we've booked the understudies for a performance."

"Whose idea was that?"

"I'll take credit for that one. Edward loves the theater."

"Nice." She took in Ash's half smile and it melted her heart. How he cared so much for Edward that he wanted to do this for him.

They almost got into an eye lock, as his met hers for words unsaid, but she lowered hers in the nick of time.

While she'd engaged in secret fantasies about him ever since the mentorship, she'd spent those years as sure as he was that a genuine relationship wasn't in the cards for her. He was just an ideal, a fever dream, a parallel universe, an *if only*. After watching her mother's life reduced to a dreary existence as Annie's father hurt his wife again and again with his cheating and lies, there could never be anything real for her. She wasn't going to do a next-gen version of her mother's sadness and inertia. She'd had one dip into the dating pool and it had turned out exactly as she thought it would, with her hurt, humiliated and left alone.

"Invitations are out for all of these events, but I don't know the status," Ash said while back to tapping into his keyboard.

No wonder he wanted her to come in for this project. This was complex. He was right when he'd said he should have kept it in house from the beginning. All of the events managers were busy all the time. She agreed with his idea that they needed to create a position that would oversee everything the team did. A job she did want to talk to him about at the right time. After all, she was great at her position, had produced at least a hundred events for EJ. There was more than celebrations. Edward was involved in many educational and charitable organizations so the calendars were constantly full.

"Got 'em," she verified the emails Ash sent through to her inbox. "For the show, a cocktail reception before and a late-night dinner after?"

"That will be up to you."

"Nothing has been planned for this?"

"I don't know."

"It's kind of late in the game."

"I guess you'll have to work some miracles."

She snickered.

"Ready for the next one?"

"Sure."

"For about thirty close friends and family we're doing a cooking class with Chef Mino Greco, pasta making in Little Italy."

"The celebrity chef? How did you get him?"

"Money, of course. Lots and lots of money.

Yes, my idea, as well. And by the way, he's supposed to be a real pain to work with."

"Oh, terrific." She made some notes. "And then the fourth event is the gala. Benefiting Edward's teenage summer work program."

"Black tie, a formal retirement dinner with five hundred guests, sit-down meal, entertainment, live auction, speeches."

"Invitations are out for all of these dates?"

"Thankfully."

"And you have RSVPs coming in?"

"I think we at least have the guest lists in good shape. I emailed that to you."

"Wow." She leaned back in her chair and mentally replayed everything Ash had just outlined. She had her work cut out for her.

CHAPTER THREE

ONCE THEY STARTED digging into further details about the charity gala, they didn't lift their heads for several hours. There were auction donations to sort through and table sponsors to verify. A pot of coffee, several glasses of ice water, and a fruit, nut and chocolate platter had been keeping them going, but they were losing steam.

"I'm starved," Ash eventually proclaimed, just as Annie was thinking the same thing.

Stretching her back, she laced her fingers behind her head. "Do you usually have food delivered?" He watched her stretching maneuver. She realized the move jutted her chest forward. She was aware of his eyes on her.

He didn't speak for a minute but finally said, "Let's have dinner at the Garden Room at Hotel Fifth and we can have a look at the Empire Ballroom while we're there. Get you acquainted." The location of the gala was in the most elegant, still-in-operation historic hotel in New York. The Garden Room was one of the hotel's formal dinner restaurants.

Annie hadn't been sure they were even going to leave the penthouse tonight, especially after they'd put noses to the grindstone and gotten to work. Let alone go out to a fancy restaurant. "I don't know if I have anything to wear. All I brought were suits." Ash's proposal made sense, to give her a look at the ballroom as the gala would surely be the crowning event of this elaborate farewell Ash had planned for Edward. But she hadn't brought dressy clothes and was wary about what other women would be wearing. Thank you, Jack, for making her self-conscious about her *Corporate Cathy wardrobe*, as he'd called it. Jack, the exception to her rules who had reinforced her decision never to fall for a man again.

"You'll wear a suit. Is half an hour enough time to get ready? I'll call the restaurant."

"Sure." As she got up and walked toward the office door, she had a sense his eyes were following her although she couldn't be sure. The last couple of hours had been a respite from thinking about him and analyzing his every move. For which she was grateful. He'd never know that he was always on her mind and in her heart, the make-believe Ash Moretti who could lift them both out of the pit of distrust and convictions that ruled their lives. She really had no clue who the real Ash was other than a good and smart leader who would certainly take EJ into the future generations.

Within fifteen minutes she was done slipping into a navy suit of blazer and pants, a gray blouse with a high neckline and her navy medium heels. Dull as dirt indeed, but dark suits were her uniform. Basically, it was easiest to dress like a businessman did. And the Denver finance industry wasn't exactly the fashion capital of the world. Slipping on a pair of gold stud earrings, she then brushed her hair and repositioned her headband. If she'd known they were going to go out to a hotel dining room, she'd have at least brought a dress. In reality, when she and Ash had made the plan on the phone, she'd pictured them being in EJ's Wall Street office all weekend, with her staying at a corporate hotel.

She made her way through what really was

a long corridor with the other guest rooms, the lounge area, the office. She paced in the living room which was the junction, not brave enough to approach his bedroom to tell him she was ready.

Soon enough he made his entrance. He had that edgy toughness to his face, the lines that he'd had even as a young man had gotten more furrowed over the years. Battle scars, in a way. They made him all the more attractive in her opinion, yet he was clearly holding on to pain. "Shall we?"

"I'm ready."

At Hotel Fifth, the French Renaissance landmark on Fifth Avenue, the Garden Room was on the twelfth floor. Not a skyscraper by any accounting, the hotel was instead old-timey elegance. A tuxedoed maître d' greeted them at the entrance. "Mr. Moretti, how nice to see you." Was Ash a regular here? Was Annie just yet another woman who'd been shown across the dining room to a premiere table centered in the dining room's outdoor gardens, lit to display their lush beauty even into the night? The maître d pulled out Annie's chair and they sat. "Welcome, *madame*. Enjoy your meal."

The restaurant was breathtaking. It was no wonder it had remained one of New York's favorites for decades. It was essentially a greenhouse, all glass with the necessary steel to hold it together. Glass walls, doors and ceilings. Outside on the other side of the glass was every colorful flower in the world, arranged in huge swaths of blossoms. There was a bonsai court and an herb garden. Small trees were full with fall foliage—everywhere Annie looked an orange or yellow leaf fluttered to the ground. Lit by the moon and fairy lights strung throughout. It was quite possibly the most romantic place she'd ever been. And she was here with the only person she would have ever wanted to come with.

And it was important to remember that he'd brought her here because they were going to look at the ballroom later. Part of the job she was doing for him! Because they were coworkers. Nothing more. She needed to give herself a crash course in *coworkers only* because being face-to-face with him was turning out to be a challenge she hadn't been prepared for. A crush on the boss never worked out; in this case it could shatter her to pieces.

A waiter in a white uniform jacket appeared

instantly. Ash wasted no time. "A bottle of the Camu Cabernet, a dozen Maine Belons on the half shell and two prawn cocktails." He shifted his eyes to Annie. "Is there anything you don't eat?"

"No."

He continued to the waiter, "For an entrée let's have the grass-fed filet medallions with the celeriac macaroni and cheese and grilled broccolini." For a kid from New Jersey, he surely grew up to live a big-city life. Whereas she chose to keep things quiet. Although he was sarcastic about the grandeur of his apartment, saying that he never entertained or had houseguests. It wasn't clear how satisfying the power of wealth was for him.

Once the waiter nodded and then disappeared Annie quizzed, "Just like that. You ordered off the top of your head." He was a paradox that intrigued her.

"Don't most hotel restaurants have more or less the same menu? It wasn't that hard to think of what sounded good after working all day."

"Do you eat here regularly?"

"EJ has used the ballroom here for a few banquets so I guess they know us around here."

"You've come a long way, Ash." She was sorry she'd said that as soon as it fell out of her mouth. It could have been construed as a sort of insult. She wasn't sure if, or how, she'd bring up their past, or if she even needed to. But if he was considering her for a promotion that would bring her back to New York she figured there would have to be some kind of recap at some point. Working as one of his VPs, she figured they'd get to know each other more than they had in that fleeting year they'd spent together. "You should be really proud of yourself."

"Yes, I told you. I've become an old bachelor with too much money and nothing to do but work."

"Old? We're both thirty-two. And think of what you've accomplished. You're about to run EJ." His bemused look made her question to herself if he had people in his life other than Edward who made sure his feet touched the ground. Who reminded him that his hard work had paid off. "Edward gave us a start, but look what you've done with it."

"You mean in spite of what in pop-speak would be called *my obstacles*."

"You and the rest of the world. Everybody has a cross to bear."

Though she knew his hurdles had been quite a bit more significant than average.

The waiter returned with the wine. Within seconds an assistant waiter laid down the plump oysters on an iced platter and the classic prawn cocktails, six large pink prawns hung old-school on the edge of a footed glass, served atop a small plate, with a silver pot of horseradish sauce for dipping.

"As I recall, you didn't have an easy road yourself."

"I didn't." That had been something that connected them in the first place. When they were twenty-two and in the mentorship program, they had founded their kinship on the fact that they'd both crawled their way out of dysfunctional families, and been left bloody and wounded.

Oh, how well she remembered that time with him. Standing around in the snack room, or going out for a beer when they'd quit work for the night. "I think we both felt like imposters on Wall Street. Kids like us who limped through the door just in time didn't necessarily get far. We didn't see in ourselves what Edward saw in us."

Ash got very still, like she had stunned him. "I haven't thought about it that way in a long time." His usually clear eyes became glassy for a moment. His soul left the table.

"Ash." She hadn't intended that, didn't think her words would have hit so hard. All she could think of was to bring him back. "I'm sorry. Did I say something wrong?"

In a snap, all of him returned to the table. He grabbed a prawn from the appetizers in front of him and took a couple of bites. Then he stopped again. And his gaze latched on to hers, looking deep into her eyes, so far that he prodded her inside, he made the restaurant disappear. "Thing were so different then," he finally said in a hushed tone. "I didn't have all of the information."

She had no idea what he was talking about but sensed she shouldn't ask. If he wanted to say more, he would.

"You like your appetizers?" Ash alternated between eating his own seafood and watching Annie eat. If he let himself, he had seconds, maybe longer, to enjoy watching her slurp down an oyster from the half shell or crunch into a piece of juicy shrimp. Her mouth was pretty. He found himself picturing bringing his lips to hers, beating out the food to the privilege.

"Delicious. There's nothing like East Coast shellfish."

His mind was elsewhere.

She'd stated aloud that they were both unlikely candidates to have found their way into Edward's mentorship program ten years ago. Because she'd opened that door, he wanted to share more. In fact, she was his witness, one he had never been ready to face. Now with him reaching his pinnacle by becoming CEO, he wanted to talk to her more, not about the trivialities of what region had the best fish or even about the retirement events, even though that was the reason Annie sat across from him tonight.

"A minute ago you made reference to the people we were at twenty-two. What were you remembering?" He'd pulled away when she'd said it, as if it was too much, but after composing himself from the knee-jerk reaction that any defensive kid would have, he found he welcomed her inquiry. He'd bottled up so many emotions inside. It was that simpatico that they'd found in one another a decade ago that had made their connection so profound.

"You mean about us."

"We connected. That's rare." Of course he remembered the Christmas party and before that, that time spent in the cabin by the lake. It was why he'd still sometimes look for her in a video meeting. She was a guidepost, evidence of what he'd never forget. "I think we shared some truths. We saw something in each other that made that safe."

Yet it had been clear that year they'd gone as far as they could with each other. There would be no enduring romantic relationship, not even a lifelong friendship. She'd gone back to Denver and they'd seen each other here and there for work. Yes, on occasion he'd wondered about more. If she would have been open to it. If he would have.

"I remember meeting you," she mused. Indeed, through the ice-breakers games in the first days of the program, he'd noticed the pretty but plain girl in cheap clothing who gave one-word answers when questioned about anything. "I didn't think I was the type who would get accepted for the mentorship.

I didn't have educated parents—I wasn't familiar with New York…"

"You must have had a good résumé from college and written a good essay as part of the application."

"It felt like a miracle that I'd even heard about the program from a college professor who encouraged me to apply."

Ash picked up the small bread basket on the table and offered her a slice before taking one himself. He was eager to know who Annie was now. What she'd gotten over and what still held her back. "If it's not too personal, what were you facing at home then? You never really told me other than that you didn't have a happy childhood." At twenty-two they'd hinted at their pain, but neither had been able to articulate it in straightforward terms. Yet it was something they definitely shared, and that set them apart from the others, at least as far as what met the eye.

She sat taller in her chair, looking like she'd made a decision. "My father habitually cheated on my mother," she began. "She'd kick him out of the house, swearing it was forever. Then a few weeks later he'd apologize and promise it would never happen again.

And she'd let him move back home, until he did it again. Over and over."

"I remember that you and I were twenty-two-year-old kids convinced we'd never get married or have children. What do you think about all that now?"

She took a sip of wine. "I tried a relationship a few years ago. It ended in disaster."

"Whoa, that's harsh. Who was he?"

"His name is Jack. He's a financial advisor in Denver."

"What happened?"

"He did the same things to me as my father did to my mother. Cheated on me. Made me feel bad about myself, unattractive. And then he'd promise to never do any of it again, beg me for a second chance."

"Did you give him one?"

"I was a sucker. I gave him four."

Ash noticed a squiggly feeling rise in him on confirming that Annie was, in fact, single. And another emotion that might have been jealousy that she'd given any of herself to another man. Then a roar at this Jack. For hurting her, Ash could become a fighting man.

A busboy arrived to clear the appetizer

plates as the waiter delivered the entrées. Ash waited for them to be alone again.

"Are your parents still doing the same routine?"

"She finally divorced him. That was actually right after the mentorship program, when my younger brother went away to college. After twenty-five years."

"What's your situation now? Are you close with them?"

"My dad died a couple of years later. He'd shriveled up into nothing. Despite all the chaos he created, he wasn't really a full person without my mom."

"Do you think he regretted cheating on her?"

"Sure. It ruined his life. And hers. And our family's. The fool."

They were quiet for a bit as they ate and the words swirled around the table all these years later like insects in a swarm. He'd known that she'd been a kid from an unhappy home, just as he'd been. He'd wondered what it would have been like if their upbringings had turned them into people determined to have healthy relationships, to do it over that way, instead of the way they chose, no relationships at all.

"How's your mom now?"

"She's okay, though she let it define her. I always wished she'd find herself a good man, but she was left too torn up. We all were. My older brother has already been divorced twice and my younger one, like me, prefers to go it alone."

"I'm genuinely sorry, Annie."

"What about you? I remember you had a challenging relationship with your father?"

"That's a polite way of phrasing it. Did I ever tell you what he said when I told him I applied for the EJ mentorship program after I read about it in a guidance counselor's office?"

"I don't think so."

"That it didn't matter because I was never going to amount to anything."

Her face fell as he fought to not let his do the same. The hundreds of wounds on his body all hurt at once. He was still the little boy beaten for spilling soup on the dining room carpet. He was still the adolescent, hormones forcing critical words out of his mouth that earned him weekends grounded at home while the other boys went to video arcades and pizza parlors. He was that young man who, despite being terrible at exams, managed to do enough extra-credit work to get one of EJ's twenty slots for mentorship.

"And now?" She put her fork down and looked at him with a sympathy that was almost humiliating. They were in their thirties and the past only mattered as much as they let it. He wasn't used to revealing his inner life to anyone, not even Edward who only knew about his circumstances in general terms. Ash was the Wall Street hotshot who made himself, and his clients, a ton of money with his ability to stay on top of trends, analyze wisely, and certainly to do it all legally, friendlily and correctly. His ability to push away his past was the very key to his success. Yet somehow around Annie he wanted to share everything he'd thought or felt in the past ten years, although he wouldn't. Especially not the most important thing.

"My fath...my father died five years ago."

Vibration surrounded their table as they both seemed to need private thoughts. Ash had a memory of sitting with Annie in a cabin in the Adirondacks, the meet and greet weekend for that year's program cohorts. It was free time between team building activities.

A group that didn't know what to do with

themselves had stood outside in a chat circle. *Where are you from? If EJ offered you a job, what department are you most interested in?* And so on. Ash had noticed Annie looking down and not saying much. It had seemed like the other mentees had gone to prestigious schools or had snazzy recommendations to the program. They'd talked about vacations in sunny destinations and parents with advanced degrees. He'd noticed Annie's clothes were worn, as were his.

Later, hanging out in the cabin, Ash and Annie had coincidentally sat close together on a bed, with their backs propped up against the wood-paneled wall and their legs outstretched. Very casual. Some of the other mentees had been outside playing volleyball. Ash had been able to hear them congratulating each other on good kills and calling the score out loud.

"I don't know how I even got into this program," he'd blurted to her, surprising himself by saying the words out loud when he'd meant to keep them to himself.

"Me, either." His hunch that they had something in common was emerging. "The college career counselor told me that if I did a lot of volunteer hours I'd look like I was serious. I put in loads of free time at a food bank for people in need. Which was easy because it meant less time I had to spend at home." For Ash, there'd been no going away to a leafy campus filled with high achievers. He'd gone to the state university, a forty-minute drive from their house.

Annie had adjusted herself from the way they were sitting side by side so that she could face him and their eyes could meet. "It was messed up at my house, too."

"How did you find EJ?" He'd instantly admired whatever determination had gotten her into the mentorship.

"I got really lucky that I had a professor who believed in me and she guided me through the whole process."

Facing each other on that bed, their knees had brushed through their jeans and Ash still remembered that sensation. Touching her, even so lightly and so innocently had affected him. He had been able to smell the citrus of her shampoo. She'd worn her hair longer then, to the elbow, whereas now it grazed her shoulders. He'd been with a few girls in college but nothing serious. He'd sensed it could be different with Annie, though. Which had immediately warned him not to get too close. He'd been hurt enough to last a lifetime.

Now here Ash was in the Garden Room all these years later but with the woman who brought all of that past back. He again heard the sounds of the volleyball game outside. Felt the squishiness of the pillow he'd been leaning against. And most especially was aware of the way the bone of Annie's knee had pressed into his own. The memory of that touch gave him the strength to say, "When I got accepted, he wanted to know if I cheated my way in somehow. He said he had no idea how a good-for-nothing sack of flesh like me could have gotten such an opportunity. He said I'd probably fail."

"You showed him."

"He was dead before I could." But he swallowed at Annie's leap of faith. He'd understood when he'd heard the expression that revenge was sweet.

"Where was your mom's place in all of this?"

"Good question. He flew off on rages so she was always trying to keep the peace." He'd lowered his eyes even though Annie was trying to maintain contact. "He'd be off on one of his yelling tantrums and she'd whisper in my ear that he'd had a little too much to drink, not to pay him any mind."

"She let you down, too."

"He treated her like crap. It's what she knew. My grandfather used to abuse my grandmother. Another cycle repeating."

Ash could easily still vomit at the memories. Karl Moretti was dead but would never be forgotten. He'd insured that Ash would never get close to anyone ever again because letting people in would certainly lead to betrayal.

Yet looking into Annie's bright green eyes something was changing inside him. Perhaps it was the same way he'd felt in that cabin so many warm days ago. He couldn't put his finger on it. But maybe it was hope.

CHAPTER FOUR

DURING AFTER-DINNER COFFEES, Ash and Annie's conversation turned back to the gala. After all, that was why she was there, in the middle of a spectacular restaurant made of glass in New York City. One reason she definitely wasn't there was to rehash her miserable childhood and the decisions it led her to and kept her from.

She also wasn't there to force Ash to do the same. This wasn't a forum for him to examine his own life, either, although she liked that he wanted to confide in her. After all, they had spent that vital year together, one that had shaped them and turned what could have been doom around in their favor. She could sit there all night across the table from him.

Sure, they could keep talking as surprisingly easily as they had at twenty-two, with her staring into the vastness of his eyes that were like clear lakes. His eyes made her want—just want. Now with the maturity that time brought, together could they maybe unburden their souls, heal their inner child, align their chakras, understand their buried wisdom, dispel their anger, shed a skin? Again, she reminded herself that none of that was why she was there.

When coffee came to an end, the hotel general manager let them into the Empire Ballroom for a look. "Oh, how lovely." The room had always been known as one of the finest special occasion destinations in New York, if not the world.

"Thirty thousand square feet."

Annie took in its enormity, done in a neoclassical style with tall archways circling the room. The mammoth crystal chandeliers were raised high enough to cast a warm glow on the floors, fine Italianate marble but unpolished so as not to become slippery. "Seating capacity looks to be about seven fifty." She'd seen rooms of this size at other hotels in her territories, but perhaps none as grandly appointed as the venerable Hotel Fifth's.

"I think our guest list caps at five hundred."

"Perfect, then the areas outside of the arches

won't have to have dining setups. We'll do cocktail tables there instead so people aren't stuck in their seats all night. They'll have other areas to stand and congregate."

"Great." Ash nodded.

She didn't have to prove to him that she knew what she was doing, nor did she need his nod of approval, but she didn't mind it nonetheless. It was in the back of her mind that he had all but baited her to New York with hints about this newly formed position overseeing events for the entire company. Something she'd definitely like to hear more about.

Change was brewing in her. It had been for a while. That she was trying to scratch an itch just out of her reach. A yearning, the knowledge that she wanted more in her life and, most importantly, that she was waiting for it. She needed to push through what held her back, needed to take change out of the theoretical and into the real.

She quickly tallied how many dining tables were out in the ballroom at the moment, probably left configured from the previous event. "How is your guest list arranged?"

"Arranged?" He looked at her, not understanding.

"I'm just trying to envision whether we'll want dining tables to seat eight, ten or twelve. Is the list separated by EJ employees, clients, family, and so on?"

"I have no idea how Marissa left that. I'll get the information for you."

"Good. Has the menu been set? Are you doing passed hors d'oeuvres?"

"I again have no idea and will get that to you right away."

If she was ever going to break out and move forward, the time had come. The stars had aligned. Opportunity was about to come face-to-face with intention.

On the outside of the archway, dozens upon dozens of empty coupe glasses were lined up next to an empty champagne fountain. Which gave her a brainstorm. "Since we have this nice outer rim for pre- and post-dinner socializing, instead of the typical champagne fountain, let's do a wine flight of fountains."

"That sounds great. But what are you talking about?" They both smiled with a little laugh. Wow, he needed to keep that smile away from her. That was the kind of smile that could make a girl question the absolutes that had defined her. His smile wasn't just cute and sincere, it was crooked. Devilish. A smile she didn't see much of in the serious business of EJ and their clients' money.

That was okay. She was getting this special piece of him right now. The private place she'd glimpsed into back then, but never dared to dream she'd come in contact with again. Thank heavens Ash didn't know that her one attempt at a boyfriend, Jack, had that same lopsided smile. That his appeal to her was that he reminded her of... *Check yourself, Annie. You're here to work.*

"We'll set up five fountains, each with different types of wine. We'll have a white, a rosé, then some reds—light and dark and darker still. Guests can float around the room tasting different selections."

"That sounds interesting."

"You know the theory that a little alcohol helps arms raise those auction paddles." It was a charity gala, after all, as per Edward's request. "Do you know particular guests that are wine connoisseurs? We can call on them to sponsor a fountain. Is it in your guest notes?"

"I've never seen guest notes."

"Hobbies, names of grandchildren, food allergies, you know."

She knew that she was good at her job. Her mind spun backward. At the end of the mentorship program, Edward had met with each of the mentees and, if they'd done a good job with him throughout the year, he'd offered them a position. Annie had picked event planning because there was an opening in Denver and, at the time, she'd thought she wanted to stay near her family.

Plus, she and Ash had had their Christmas fling and had agreed that nothing further was to come of it between them. Yet truth be told, she'd pined for him until the program ended and she'd never stopped, a fact he would have no inkling of. She intended to keep it that way. Settling into a life far away from him had seemed the smartest move. She hadn't been going to take a risk that he'd turn out to be like her father. Her plan had been to take no chances.

They made their way into the center of the ballroom and onto the smooth hardwood dance floor which had a certain kind of hush when empty. To the side there was a stage for a midsize band to play. The largest of the room's chandeliers delineated the area. All of the lighting was just perfect, a mix of golden and rosy glows that would make everyone look good.

In the middle of the palatial and ornate ballroom she and Ash turned in a circle, taking it all in. They stood close, side by side. So close that she could imagine him sweeping a long arm around her waist and pulling her to him in until their bodies were touching. In fact, this wasn't the first time she'd envisioned something like that. Here, being next to him where she'd wanted to be for so long, no one could blame her for being taken over by the fantasy of dancing with him.

His body would feel warm and firm pressed against hers. With his other hand, big and bold, he'd take hers, and their elbows would crook in waltzing posture. And then the music would rise up around them and their eternity would be locked, certain, and neither would ever drop the other's hand. They'd dance from this lifetime into the next and the one after.

She took a step backward as if the proximity was what was causing her to have such inappropriate thoughts. With a few full breaths into her core, she noticed the magnificent staircase that led down to the ballroom from the main lobby, the steps marble and swathed in garnet-colored carpet flecked with gold.

"The staircase. One hundred percent fairy tale." The bannisters were mahogany, carved into an S shape and polished to a gleam. "This ballroom is Cinderella level."

"Did you expect any less?" Ash teased.

She had a split second—okay, a split two seconds—of picturing herself as a guest at a grand ball, in a gown, maybe sapphire blue, fitted in the bodice then full from the waist, leading down to a train in the back, perhaps tulle with sapphire crystals. Her long hair— in reality, hers grazed her shoulders but in the fantasy it was, of course, long, thick, wavy and swept up into an elaborate do, curls pinned just so to look somehow like a biblical virgin, a sexy bride and a stately princess all at once. A necklace with a huge sapphire accentuated by small diamonds would grace her throat.

By her side would be this epic man in a tuxedo, and she'd have her arm through his to ensure her safe passage down the stairs and into the ballroom.

Real life please, Annie. Over dinner, Ash

had reminded her of time passed, of that day at that cabin when she'd first experienced what it was to reveal herself to someone. She'd never figured on sharing her feelings, and hearing someone else's. That hadn't been done in her family, hadn't been safe. Invariably, someone would bring them up later, use them to mock.

Neither Annie nor Ash had really revealed much back then, but even the brush with vulnerability had been both scary and cathartic. Then there had been the months between the retreat and the Christmas party. They'd worked hard in the program, learning corporate structure and about serving clients in the financial sector. All along, they couldn't deny that an unexpected bond grew between them.

One would save a place at the communal dinner for the other. When they had unscheduled time they'd bopped around New York. He'd known the city well and had showed her lots of fun on a budget. Slices of pizza so big it had taken two hands to hold them. Free days at museums. Walking around Coney Island imagining what the old days of New York were like.

Then that night of the holiday party, her in

that cheap red dress, when they hadn't been able to hold back what was bursting from both of them.

Now, in the center of the ballroom she turned to face him, not making a decision to do so, instead it was a phenomenon derived from its own power. They stared into each other's eyes, that echo of the empty dance floor the only sound. Ever so gradually, millimeter by millimeter, the gravitational pull brought their faces toward each other's, hers up to his and his down to hers. As if they were in slow motion. Until there was only a bit of air between them. The tiniest wisp separating their mouths. Until finally, there wasn't and their lips touched.

Annie had thought about this moment for so long. What it would be like to kiss him again. It wasn't with the high pulse of youth and cocktails and mistletoe. No, this kiss was sober with gravity and maturity. He tilted his head slightly to the right, hers following to the left. A second kiss lingered longer, much longer, as though neither wanted to give up the plush berth of each other. Before she'd had a chance to think about it and maybe opt out, her arms floated up around his neck and she felt the press of his solidness against her.

It was a hallucination, she was sure of it. Nothing in real life could have felt that good. Then Ash did the unthinkable. He wrapped his long arms around her waist just like in her fantasy and brought her in even closer to him. Which meant her heart was in big, big trouble.

As he swiped the elevator fob to rocket Annie to the penthouse, Ash had no idea how they'd actually gotten from the ballroom of Hotel Fifth to here. He was only sure of one thing. His feet hadn't touched the ground along the way. His mind replayed the scene over and over again. In the middle of the dance floor, one minute they were talking about wine fountains and the next minute they were kissing.

Once they stepped into the apartment, the air was thick with apprehension. He immediately second-guessed his innocent assumption that it would be fine, and convenient, to have Annie stay with him while she was here. But he'd never imagined that what just happened was going to happen!

He'd certainly had no intention of it. Yet all

of a sudden his lips had been touching hers. Lost in a swirl of not one, not two, but a mass of kisses, a vortex his body told him he could continue for hours. Finally, they'd pulled apart from each other and sort of giggled at the unexpected impulse. Annie had touched her fingers to her own mouth in a sort of *oops* gesture. "Where did that come from?"

"I have no idea." They'd both shrugged. Obviously they hadn't been going to debate it in the empty ballroom of Hotel Fifth. "Let's go home." And he'd uttered *let's go home* as if it was perfectly routine.

As he closed the front door, effectively locking them in for the night, was it time to unpack those kisses further? "Just to be clear…"

"Yeah, absolutely. I got swept up in the moment and…"

"Silly. A ballroom with a grand staircase. Like a fairy ta…"

"I hope I didn't…"

"No, not at all…"

"We did have that…when we were younger…"

"It was a long time ago and we knew neither of us wanted…"

"I mean, obviously, we…"

"Were clear from the beginning..."

Annie stopped to make a decision before she spoke. "It's been a long day that started in Denver for me. I'd like to go to sleep."

"Yes." Disappointment coursed through him. Illogically, he wanted to plop down on one of his couches with her, maybe her curling her feet under her legs while he stretched his out on the coffee table. And from there they'd chat about normal things, their days, the news, something they'd observed. Just like couples did when they got home. He'd never been part of a couple so all of those were notions he only occasionally thought of. Although more so lately, he had to admit.

He walked her down the long hallway. She could have found it on her own—she hardly needed escorting. Yet he wanted to. What he was aching to do was to kiss her again. Just a good-night peck. Just one. Or maybe twelve.

When they'd had that night ten Christmases ago, he hadn't let himself dwell on it too much afterward. He'd already reasoned out that caring and closeness meant you trusted someone, and then that someone would certainly harm you in the end. Maybe, just maybe, Karl...his father, would watch a ball game on television with Ash and listen as he shared his dreams of playing sports. But by the end of the night, Ash would be assured that he shouldn't try out for the school's team because he threw like a wimp and would never be chosen.

Ash had so many examples of hope and vulnerability being taken advantage of, he'd learned to stop trying. He knew he'd always stay in his self-protective shell. No risks. And it seemed that Annie's intention was the same. On occasions, he'd thought about her over the past ten years. If things had been different.

"Good night." He backed away. Now that they'd kissed at the ballroom, he had to immediately start backtracking from that error. Things weren't different for him. Her, either. She'd agreed, other than a bad experience with one other man.

"See you in the morning."

Ash rose early and the first thing he wondered was whether Annie was still asleep in the guest room and whether she'd slept well. He reached for his phone and snarled to find three texts from Zara that had come through in the middle of the night.

Hi, Ash. Hope we're still on for drinks after work. You promised!

He'd certainly never said yes to any of her invitations, in fact, the sound of her voice was babble to him so he rarely even recalled whatever nonsense she spewed.

I made a date with Tajar and Shirin for a drive out to their country house this weekend. You'll love it!

How would she know what he loved or didn't?

Thinking of you, Pookie!

Pookie? Was that a word? He was most definitely not her Pookie. And why did every text end with an exclamation point?

Zara must have thought that by bombarding him with her presence she would wear him down and that eventually he *would* be her Pookie. Which was never going to happen.

"Good morning." Annie entered the kitchen as Ash was pouring himself a cup of coffee from the pot that had been set on a timer.

He was grateful the brew was hot and fresh, and he reached for a second of the heavy ceramic mugs he favored in the morning. "How do you take it?"

"Light, no sugar please." As he poured her coffee, he noticed she was wearing a pajama set of a top and shorts that clung to her in a most appealing way. The top fit like a T-shirt and she was clearly wearing nothing underneath. And the shorts were short enough to show the entirety of her shapely legs, the skin golden like her tousled morning hair. He could tell that she hadn't made a fuss of fixing herself up for seeing him upon awakening like some women would.

When he did date or have an encounter with a woman, he was always clear that he was not open to anything ongoing. Usually, he woke in an empty bed, having ended the tryst before the light of day brought questions and possibilities. Nonetheless, on occasion, he'd wake up to find a woman he'd been with the night before looking lacquered, polished, preened and perfumed, sometimes in elaborate frilly lingerie that looked more like it belonged on a store mannequin than a real person with a pulse and a heart. Whereas Annie's naturalness fed right into a budding delusion about a kind of domesticity that felt natural and organic.

They hadn't been alone together like this in ten years, during which neither had reneged on their vow to be nothing more than friendly colleagues, lest family histories repeat themselves. Although he was needing to remind himself of that. It wasn't like he was going to be able to erase the ballroom kisses from last night. Even though he had to at least put them to the side.

He handed her a mug and took scientific reportage of their fingers gliding against each other's during the exchange. He could swear the contact made his fingertips tingle. Yet that was impossible.

"Let's run over to the Castle Theatre so you can see what we're setting up for the Broadway event." Time to punch the clock on the day, which would be a busy one and would hopefully take his mind off Annie's supple legs that he could wrap around his waist as he lifted her against him.

He made toast, which he then buttered, plated and placed in front of her on the counter with a pot of jam. She sat on one of the breakfast stools while he stood with his back against the counter.

"I was thinking about the gala. And that terrific ballroom." It certainly was terrific, as his lips remembered.

Ash looked at his phone, recalling the annoying Pookie texts. "Listen, there's another thing I want to talk to you about. I don't know if you've ever encountered Edward's stepdaughter, Zara."

"No." She spread her toast with jam. He went on to explain all of the unsolicited and unwelcome surprise visits, the calls and texts, the Pookie thing.

"I was hoping that by us working closely together, you could sort of be a buffer between me and her. Until Edward isn't coming into the office anymore."

"In what way would I be able to shield you from Zara?"

"I don't know, just your presence. Making it clear that you're a professional with no time for me to be detained by nonsense. And help me keep the way she pesters me a secret. There's a lot of gossip at the office and I don't want it to get back to Edward. She's an embarrassment I want to keep under wraps."

"Your little secret is safe with me." She didn't know about his *big* secret, but that was a different matter entirely. One he wasn't sure he'd ever tell anyone.

"I thought you could be a barrier." Ash poured two glasses of a green drink from a pitcher in the fridge and handed one to her, again as if it was the most normal thing in the world. "I'm hoping if I'm with you a lot—" that sounded even better aloud than he'd ever imagined it would "—she wouldn't dare pull her shenanigans in front of someone else."

"Doesn't your PA, Irene, know what's going on if she's continuously barging into your office? Why don't you have her fend off Zara for you?"

He sipped his drink. "Irene's been a fine PA to me but she's a gossipy little auntie. And, as I've said, I don't want this getting back to Edward."

"Okay. I'll do what I can as the situation presents itself."

"You'll stay in New York for a few weeks to help see this through?"

"I guess you need my help in person."

He was filled with relief, not to mention a jolt at the assurance that he'd be spending more time with her in person. Which he'd never felt about anyone. That was all it was, unfamiliar, so a little thrilling. None of it meant anything.

"This will all mean the world to Edward."

"Oh, so you're working a guilt tactic on me?"

They both giggled. "As long as it's effective."

"At some point I'll need to go back to Denver, lock up my house, bring some things from my office there."

"Whenever you want."

"Okay, here we go."

His gut told him that big fat ballroom kiss was going to be a factor in this strictly business relationship he needed to convince himself of.

CHAPTER FIVE

ANNIE SMILED AS she marveled at the Broadway theaters and their world-renowned marquees. New York's famed theater district was still a sight to behold. People came and went in every direction, some who probably worked or lived in the area, some tourists exploring Times Square, perhaps some who were performers or crew heading early into the theaters. "I haven't been around here in a long time," she mused. "There's a buzz that isn't like anywhere else. These old theaters look like they're standing at attention waiting for eight o'clock when the curtains rise."

"Come on." Ash had called ahead, and announced himself at the box office of the Castle Theatre. A worker let them in by unlocking one of the framed etched-glass entrance doors and quickly latching it shut once they stepped inside. The interior was empty in midmorning other than the sound of vacuum cleaners being operated by two custodians. Ash walked Annie into the lobby.

She read from her phone, "This theater was opened in 1903 and the lobby is done in the Art Nouveau style." She pointed out the vine tendril stone carvings on the walls. "It has such a different feel in here from when there's a performance and people are filling the seats."

Ash smiled at her enthusiasm. "That's why I thought of this event. I realized that even the most privileged people never get to experience having a theater all to themselves."

"You're good at my job, Ash," she laughed. "It must be costing you a bloody fortune."

"It'll be a gift from me and some of the other most senior people at EJ. Edward goes to the theater at least once a week. He helps keep Broadway in business."

She loved that he'd thought to plan an evening around something so dear to Edward's heart. "What a special memory you're creating for him."

"There are usually no performances on Mondays. So that's when we were able to rent it out and hire the understudies. It gives them a nice chance for an extra performance."

"Do you remember when we came to Broadway to see that musical ten years ago? Again with Edward's generosity. He wanted the mentees to see a Broadway show as some of them, like me, had never seen one, never even been to New York. What was the name of that silly show about people in an office?"

"*Desk Work*."

"Right."

He brought her upstairs to the large mezzanine lobby. "This is the party space."

She took in the dimensions and decor. Massive insect wings done in cast iron adorned the walls, giving a flow to the area, dark carpet guiding people to enter through the doors to the seating. "Gorgeous. Let's do fun hors d'oeuvres up here. We can do charcuterie cups. And a global thing. We'll do a dim sum dumpling, a tiny taco, a samosa. And colorful cocktails like a lemon spritz."

"You're making me hungry."

When they were done, Ash ushered Annie into the car and the driver pulled away from the curb and into traffic. Ash had slid in right next to her, making her aware of their legs pressed against each other atop the beige leather of the seat. Her dress pulled up on her thigh a bit when she sat. And she couldn't stop focusing on the feel of Ash's coarse black jeans on her bare leg. She'd spent a third of her life dreaming of little moments like this. Being in close physical contact with him. Working on something together, huddled, in their own personal world.

Oh, how she'd fantasized about him leering at her the way he had in the kitchen this morning as he poured her coffee, his eyes making a titillatingly slow trek down her pajama-clad body. She'd worked hard not to let the effect his eyes had on her whole body show. In reality, she'd been tingling from head to toe. It was a thrill she'd waited for, although never believing it was actually going to transpire.

Annie wasn't the type of woman men stared at. With her Sensible Suzy clothes, another insult from Jack. It was confusing for her. Sometimes the fact that men didn't notice her left her feeling lonely, but at the same time keeping herself from the attention of bad men like her father was prudent.

She knew through media coverage that Ash kept company with some of the most beautiful women in the world. Stylish New York women that turned heads wherever they went. But that ogle this morning had been unmistakable.

Although just like the ballroom kisses last night, nothing ongoing was to come of any of that. Her inner self could enjoy it, but then she needed to put it on a shelf with the rest of her memorabilia about him.

That was probably not going to be as easy as it sounded.

After visiting the theater, they went to the office to pick up all the paperwork that had already been generated regarding the events. "I haven't had occasion to be in the New York office for over two years." And Annie hadn't walked through the doors with Ash in a decade. As soon as she did, recollections flooded her.

"Welcome back."

"That glass conference room is where Edward holds the Wednesday meetings." It had gotten an update with bright geometric art. They walked past the small kitchen where, a decade past, she'd made herself cups of tea. She'd made one for Ash too, every time. And whenever she'd put the cup down on his small desk he'd given her a look of appreciation that had made her gush inside. Like he hadn't been able to believe the kindness of her gesture.

As they headed toward the communal room, she peeked down the row of cubicles to the right to find The One. It was the last in its row and the closest to the wall. While anyone assigned it as their workspace would be within their rights to complain that it was dark and a bit isolated, that night at the Christmas party it had been perfect. No, it hadn't had the comfort and luxuries offered at a five-star hotel, but they wouldn't have noticed even if it had. After an autumn of fighting a scary attraction to each other because they both were afraid to let anyone close, they couldn't deny that something genuine was at play between them.

And there it had been, stupid Christmas, without one happy childhood memory for either of them. And her stupid dowdy red dress. And the stupid eggnog that tasted like dessert but was a killer of inhibitions. And then the stupidest of stupid, the branch of mistletoe that the office manager had hung above a doorway. Ash and Annie had passed through the threshold to get another eggnog and they

ANDREA BOLTER 99

had looked up to the leaves, stems and tiny berries. They had both shrugged as if they were going to go ahead and kiss like it was no big deal.

Annie had wanted to escape into happy new year promises and joy. And she had wanted to know something that she hadn't yet had, and had been a hundred percent sure that she wanted to know it with Ash. Their long-term unavailability had made it actually seem a safe prospect. She hadn't realized that ten years later she'd continue to remember every moment of it, that it would haunt her for the rest of her life. Along with what might have been.

After the kiss under the mistletoe, they hadn't been able to hold back one more day and had spontaneously stolen away from the party. Reaching for each other's hand, they'd careened down the dark cubicle row, running to find a place with acceptable privacy.

"Here," she had said. Then, in the shadow of the few dim lights still on in that part of the office, they'd culminated what had been building for months.

Desperate hands and hungry mouths, young bodies coursing with adrenaline, they had dizzied each other in an urgent frenzy. So much so that Annie didn't think he'd even noticed her little wince of pain, the one that meant she'd always remember Ash and New York for moving her into a new state of being.

Now, back in the office with Ash, Annie exchanged pleasantries with his PA and other people on the floor. "Irene, how are you? Trevor, nice to see you. Hi, Shantae." Everything was so shiny about the New York office. Ultramodern, sleek metal and hard plastic furniture, everything done in chrome and white with accents of slate blue, and potted trees to give it life.

From the execs coming in and out of glass-enclosed offices to the interns who moved wherever they were needed, everyone looked motivated and polished. To say that the Denver office was more basic was an understatement. Annie was again in one of her drab *uniforms* of a navy dress with her hair held back with her ever-present headband. She even garnered a couple of quizzical once-overs from some super stylish women passing by. This was New York City. Wall Street. More than just one street in reality, the district was known the world over as where money was managed, made and lost. The financial heartbeat of the United States. People dressed accordingly.

As they walked toward his office, Irene gestured to the waiting area, "Ash, Zara is here."

Annie knew the look on Ash's face was exasperation, as he'd told her what a nuisance Edward's stepdaughter had become. He quickly brought her and Zara into his office and closed the door behind them, not wanting Zara to say anything embarrassing out there in the bullpen of snoop and gossip.

"Pookie!"

Annie had to bite her lip to keep from laughing. Ash was no one's Pookie and called no one Pookie. As silly as it was, though, she had a tinge of jealousy and thought to herself that if anyone was going to be his Pookie, she'd want it to be her. Zara finally took actual notice of Annie. "Who's this?"

Annie stuck out her hand for a shake, as people did in an office. Zara looked at her like she was horrified at the prospect and eyed her for a once-over. Zara was over-the-top in a tiny tweed suit, the skirt no bigger than a sticky note and the jacket opened so low it looked as though she might not be wearing a top underneath. But at least she had a style, as did the other women Annie observed in the office pool. Annie felt like a Plain Jane in the dress she'd worn, with its high collar and knee-length skirt. There was nothing wrong with it, it just had no pizzazz.

Ash didn't seem to be the slightest bit interested in what anyone was wearing. "Zara, this is Annie Butterfield from the Denver office. She's going to be taking over the retirement events."

"A-ash, I thought I was going to be your right-hand woman," Zara said with a wink.

"No. Zara, Annie is the best events planner EJ has ever had and she'll be taking over. May I also remind you that this is a place of business and you and I have no actual business together? There is no reason for you to come to the office every day. Is anything about that unclear?"

Annie admired that Ash kept his voice steady even though she could tell he was reaching his wits' end.

"You know why I come every day, Ash-y. It's to see you."

"That's very flattering. But you need to stop."

Wow, she came to the office every day? Annie could understand how that must be a nuisance.

"Did you think about going to Tajar and Shirin's beach house with me?"

"No, Zara."

"How about dinner at Skirted? I hear that's the most popular place in town right now."

"No, Zara."

"Why don't we do something wild, like fly to Paris for the weekend?"

He looked over to Annie. He'd asked her to help buffer him from Zara, but what did he want her to do? Maybe as they got into a rhythm she could be a lookout and not let Zara in to see Ash until she finally tired of these unannounced visits. But Annie had loads of work ahead of her. She wasn't going to have time to be Ash's security guard. He was going to need to be clearer as to what he expected of her.

"Zara," Ash's voice sounded like he was talking to a child. "I'll let you be the first to know what Annie and I have kept under wraps." He walked over toward Annie, and put an arm around her shoulder. Annie's brows bunched, unclear what was going on.

"Ash?" Zara questioned.

"Annie and I are together. She's my girl-friend." He leaned over and gave Annie a kiss on the cheek.

She was dumbfounded, frozen with her mouth open. In fact, she felt like she was going to turn to stone.

"Whaaaaat?" Zara shrieked.

Annie couldn't believe her ears, either. She assumed Ash was kidding and that he'd admit to the joke in a minute. Instead, he turned his face toward her wide-open eyes. He nodded his chin down and then up, motioning for her to say something, urging her on.

"Yeah," Annie squeaked out, without conviction. He wanted her to pretend to be with him? Was that the kind of buffer he had in mind when he'd first asked for her help, or did he just give birth to this brainchild? Pretend to be a couple? If only he knew what torture that would be for her. That it was an unreasonable request.

But there was so much he didn't know. Everything that had been given the night of that holiday party. Then the possible twist of fate that had lingered afterward... How after the mentorship it had been easy enough to say that she preferred to return home. That she had wanted to be with her family. Edward had agreed and back to Denver she had gone. No one had ever known that hadn't been the reason she'd left. It had been because of Ash, who was accepting a position in New York. Even though Annie had thought she'd never be in a relationship, *not* being in a relationship *with him* would be too hard. She couldn't have stayed; she'd had to go. A decision she'd second-guessed for the past decade. One that seemed to be on the verge of being raised again.

Ash, she silently pleaded. *Don't make me pretend to love you. Or pretend not to.*

"Yes, Annie and I spent a lot of time together at the Denver office." There was no truth to what Ash was telling Zara, who was snarling like an alley cat. To Annie's knowledge, Ash hadn't been to the Denver office in ages. "And, well, we fell in love." She never thought she'd hear those words come out of his mouth.

He tightened his hand around her shoulder in an exaggerated way, pulling them closer together. He gave her a squeeze, prodding her to say something.

"Yes. Ash. Love." Gibberish. She didn't want

to put those words together in a proper sentence. This was too close for comfort. Especially after they'd kissed last night. It was more than her heart could take.

Yet she wanted to help Ash, who didn't want to hurt Edward by telling him about Zara throwing herself on him, or having him hear about it from the office pipeline. This would certainly get Zara off his back. Annie owed Edward, too. Even though she hadn't reached the heights Ash had, Edward had given her a career in Denver where she had been able to buy her own home. He was a paternal figure for all of his mentees, never even knowing how badly some people like the two of them needed that.

Zara stood speechless, her thick false eyelashes coming unglued on the sides. Her pink lipstick was cakey in the corners of her open mouth.

Ash brought his hand to Annie's cheek in a caress so tender that she almost pulled away from it. He repeated her silly staccato. "Yes. Annie. Love."

Ash predicted that within hours, Zara would have told a few people at EJ that Ash was off the market and the office gossip wheel would be turning at full speed. In the case of this information, he didn't mind. He had to assume that Zara wouldn't continue to throw herself at a man that was taken. If all went according to plan, Ash's new status as a spoken-for man would allow him and Annie to come and go together at the office without it seeming strange.

Although, once Zara had left and they were alone in his office, Annie voiced her discomfort. "Where did you get the idea to say you and I were dating?"

"I just spit it out. I realized in an instant that was a way I could get her off my back."

"But now she'll tell everyone! We'll have to keep up appearances for I don't know how long."

"It's just a few weeks. Behind closed doors—" his voice slowed "—we'll know it's just make believe." Was this going to be as easy as he was trying to convince her it was? Was he so sure he could playact at something that had the potential to feel only too real? He had to.

"Alright, I'll do this for Edward's sake," Annie said. "He's such a good man. He didn't just put us on our feet, he's lifted up so many young people."

He was grateful for her loyalty. "I realize I've just sprung this on you."

"Yes, you have."

"Listen, if the situation becomes unworkable, we'll cut it right off. And I promise the VP position I've spoken about won't be in jeopardy."

"Well, thank you for that. But who's going to believe you and I are together anyway?" Annie turned to stand face-to-face with him in the center of his huge office. Well, not exactly face-to-face given he was a foot taller than her.

"Why wouldn't people believe that you and I are a couple?"

"Look at me, Ash. Let's be honest. The world would expect you to be with a knockout who has eight-foot-long legs and a daddy worth billions. Like the women you actually date."

"Notice how I'm never seen with any of them twice. Those women bore me to pieces." Annie didn't bore him. She never had.

Christmas. Ten years ago. She had been quiet and serious, didn't dress flashy, never monopolized the conversation. They'd reached into each other's depth somehow.

The holiday season had made Ash especially lonely. Perhaps it had been hearing about the plans of the cohorts in the program. Annie and he had been the only ones who weren't returning to beloved homes. One had spoken of a holiday table that would hold twelve different desserts. Another had looked forward to a vacation in the Galapagos with a family friend who was a famous marine biologist. At the party, he and Annie had been talking and looking out one of the windows. Then they'd gone into the main party room and kissed under the mistletoe. That tiny kiss had electrified him. Before he'd known it he'd taken her hand and they'd started running down the hall to a darkened area. And they'd swung into an unused cubicle.

Their mouths had smashed together, both of them taking and giving at the same time. He'd kissed her cheek, her jaw, bent to kiss the crook of her neck, the expanse of her throat. As soon as he'd started, he hadn't been able to get enough. He'd been with a couple of girls in college but had found sex inhibited and lackluster. Not with Annie. She'd met his every move, pulled at his shoulders, trying to hold his body close to hers, as close as they could be. His hands had slid to her hips where he'd pressed against her, his body already agitated, his manhood at full attention.

As he'd ground against her, she'd found his mouth for another kiss that he'd felt all the way down to his toes. Sure that no one was in that part of the office he'd lifted her up onto the desk, her legs wrapping around his waist. He'd reached to pull up her dress and glided her underwear off until he had access to her warm—no, burning hot—center. She'd undone his belt and unzipped his pants, pulling them down enough to feel his passion ready for her. He'd plunged into her. She'd twitched a little but then steadied herself. They'd been full of youth and eagerness. He'd taken her in pendulous strokes, her lifting to meet him, over and over and over until the party had disappeared.

Afterward, they'd crumbled into a pile together on the cubicle carpet, spent and, for him anyway, covered in sweat and regret. What had happened must never again. Annie wasn't a one-night kind of girl, but that was all he'd had to offer. He'd liked her so much that he hadn't wanted to hurt her, even as he'd suspected he'd already done just that by letting desire get the best of him. Never again, he'd thought even as he held her in his arms in that dark office.

After that, they'd withdrawn from each other a bit. The intimacies they'd shared could go to their graves. Time had passed; Ash had known how to compartmentalize. It was one of his survival skills. They'd completed the program, and Annie had transferred to the Denver office as she'd wanted to.

After all of their history, would he be asking too much of her now to pull off this ruse for Zara's sake? Especially after the very unfake sparks between them had led to that celestial kissing at the ballroom?

If he was being honest, it might not only be asking too much of Annie to pull off this charade. He might be asking too much of himself.

As for Annie not being a New York fashion plate... "I think you look great. But if you're concerned, do you want to bring some more clothes from Denver? Or, if you don't have the proper ones, why don't we just buy some? Do you have a gown?"

"I do, but I don't know if it's enough for a New York gala."

"There's the theater evening. The pasta making will be casual. Pajamas for the breakfast. There will be a few dinners with EJ VIPs. Do you want to go shopping?"

"What, here in New York?"

"I'll have Irene call Bergen's and make an appointment."

"An appointment?"

"Yeah, tell her what you might want and they'll pull it in advance. It'll save time." A skeptical look came across her face. "What?"

"You've sure come a long way, Ash. That's what I mean about the plausibility of us as a couple. Neither of us grew up with personal shoppers. Yet when you say it, it makes perfect sense."

"I told you before, Annie, living well is the best revenge. Now, go talk to Irene. By now she probably knows we're together," he made a quotation gesture. "We'll leave in a half hour."

Never in Ash's wildest imagination would he have thought that sitting in a private dressing room at Bergen's, the famous luxury goods store on the Upper East Side, would be as entertaining as it was. The saleswoman, Lynette, was able to merely look at Annie and know what sizes and styles would fit her best. "Mr. Moretti, would you like to have a seat?"

She pointed to a fleur-de-lis sofa with a low table in front of it that held a small coffee urn and all the necessary accompaniments. There was also a pedestaled tray that held an enticing variety of chocolates. Ash sat down as Lynette circled Annie, no doubt envisioning what would best suit both the occasions and her petite frame.

"Why don't we go with a capsule wardrobe for the more casual events?"

"What does capsule wardrobe mean?" Annie asked, taking a sip of the sparkling water she'd chosen.

"It's a collection of pieces that coordinate with each other so you can use them as needed. I've pulled some selections," Lynette said, wheeling over a rack of clothes in coordinating hues of tan, black, white and pink. She held up a pair of tan wide-leg trousers and demonstrated with other items. "For example, we can pair these with this matching knit boatneck top. Or if perhaps you're going into evening, we can use this silky black tank and pick up

the tan in this little cardigan and a gold necklace. Then the gold necklace works with this
white dress." She held each set of pieces together to demonstrate.

"That looks very New York," Annie said.
Ash supposed she meant that New York was
dressier than what she was used to, and that
may have been true. Although Annie did
travel through the West Coast and Asia for her
current position with EJ, she seemed to favor
dark suit pants and light blouses, not much
variety. It didn't matter a hoot to him but he
wanted her to feel confident and equipped to
pull off the masquerade. As Lynette guided
Annie to a changing area, Ash wondered what
the past ten years had been like for her. Trav-
eling alone, heading up all of those training
seminars as the company expanded into the
Pacific Northwest and Asia.

He had no sense of her personal life, either.
Except for one foray, she said she'd stuck to
the no-relationship rule they had both already
had in place ten years ago. Annie said there
was a man named Jack, but that he was un-
kind and that he cheated on her. Ash snarled,
wanting to punch someone he'd never met for
hurting her. What an fool this Jack must have

been. If Annie was his, Ash would never look at another woman again.

If Annie was his? Did he just think that? No one was ever going to be his!

With this new fake boyfriend thing, it would be easy to fall for the charade himself. He needed vigilance and concentration. Annie modeled a few of the outfits for him. It was unnecessary, because she was welcome to choose whatever she wanted. But he had to admit to a bit of a wicked thrill at gawking. How lovely she looked in each one. That golden hair was loose, released from the headband he'd usually seen, each strand set free to lie this way or that without having to conform to each other or work as a unit. She looked almost wantonly sexy, reminding him of that outrageous kiss at the ballroom. The one he was supposed to be forgetting.

Which wasn't going to be easy on the night of the gala, if what she was wearing as she stepped out of the dressing room was any indication. Lynette had chosen an exquisite ball gown that looked like it was spun from silk. It was a golden color that matched Annie's hair. A swath of the opaque fabric swept horizontally from shoulder to shoulder. It was fitted to the waist. The bottom part became a full princess-caliber skirt, with a train that followed her as she walked around the room checking herself out in various mirrors.

"What do you think?" she asked in such a sincere voice it made his heart ache.

"You'll be the most beautiful woman there." Did she not know how spectacular she looked? He swore his breath had stopped for a moment.

CHAPTER SIX

As a driver whirled them back to the office, Annie shuffled through the paper files on her lap. Ash was busy with something on his tablet, which wasn't enough to keep her from frequently looking over to him, taking in his magnificent profile.

The whole week of celebrations was a fitting tribute to Edward and she looked forward to making each event as memorable as she could. She had to admit she would feel more confident doing so in the clothes they'd just bought. Actually, that Ash insisted on paying for. Which was beyond charming. That whole experience had been the stuff of dreams. A personal shopper, capsule wardrobe, a magnificent gown in which she'd swirled around the dressing room, gaining Ash's approval. Moments like that didn't happen to her in

Denver. Most of the time she went about her business as if she was invisible.

She'd take a quick trip back at some point to get some more of her clothes and things from her office. After all, the supposed long weekend she'd come for had ended a couple of days ago. Yes, she was going to stay in New York to see these events through, which had now progressed to also staying at Ash's apartment and pretending to be his girlfriend.

She sneaked another glance at him. These last few days had been a whirlwind. Ash had brought her to New York, given her an incredible opportunity and bought her a new wardrobe. And, oh yeah, kissed her like their lives had depended on it. She tingled as she thought of it again, his forceful lips demanding one kiss after the next. One of them must have been the first to later declare that it had been spontaneous but wrong, and shouldn't happen again. She already couldn't remember who'd spoken those words of wisdom, her or him.

When they met Edward at the office, Ash said, "You remember Annie Butterfield from the Denver office, don't you?"

"Of course. Wonderful to see you, my dear."

"I've brought Annie to New York to help

me fete you…but also so she and I could stop having to carry out this relationship long-distance."

The news registered on Edward's face.

"Well, well, Ash, I had no idea. I'm surprised and delighted. You didn't say anything when we had lunch the other day."

Ash was caught. He covered with, "I didn't bring it up because I figured we had enough going on without adding complications."

"Quite the opposite. Our senior management and clients have always preferred that leadership has a settled personal life."

"As you've told me many times."

Ash put his arm awkwardly around Annie's shoulder again, his over-the-top pretending-to-be-a-couple pose. Annie mashed her lips together. He probably had no inkling that every time he did something like that, her insides swirled. It wasn't that easy to pretend and then not. Because the not pretending was pretend, too. The reality was that the more they acted like they were together, the more Annie saw flashes of an ongoing life with him.

"Yes, I want to see you get married, have children. Let's the three of us have dinner this week. I'm so pleased." Edward proceeded down the hallway with a youthful spring in his step.

Annie had to remind herself over and over again that there was no circumstance in which she and Ash would become a real couple even though it was something she'd gone to sleep thinking about for the past decade. A decade! Ten entire years of her life, daydreaming, night fantasizing and idly musing about the only man who'd meant anything to her.

It didn't matter though because they could pretend for Edward and Zara and the whole of New York as much as they wanted, but the reality was that Ash had never wavered in his resolution not to be in love. And she was one and done giving it a try. So even if she had the opportunity to show her love to the only man she'd ever wanted to, neither of them would see it through. Edward's words *married* and *settled* had made her bristle.

Nonetheless, they developed a routine, a platonic work-husband and work-wife sort of thing. In addition to the retirement events, both she and Ash had their other duties to oversee and the days passed quickly. An office within Ash's office had been set up for her, which meant that they need only play at their charade whenever the door was open or they were in the corridors.

As she listened to Ash on the phone, already beginning to assume the role of CEO, she wondered again where her own career might have taken her had she not been so dragged down by the toxicity in her home as a child, and especially as a teen when she became aware of what was really going on. When she'd started to understand that if her dad didn't come home at night, it wasn't because he was at work, despite how many times he or her mother would try to convince the kids of that.

Annie and her brothers knew why their mom sat at the kitchen table in the middle of the night sobbing, covering her mouth with her hand to muffle her cries. That when their father did return in the morning or the next night after his forays, their home felt like the rooms were filled to the ceiling with milk, a thick cloudy uneasiness where no one could see ahead of them. Why had it taken her mother so long to leave him? Fear, Annie supposed. Fear that being alone would be worse than living with a liar and a cheater. It left every member of their family inert, reluctant to take chances.

It had been obvious to her by the end of the

mentorship program, that even though they'd distanced themselves from each other after the holiday interlude, Ash was a danger. Everything about him was wrong for being right. With him, she had been afraid she would learn to trust. And that was something she was determined never to take a chance on, convinced it could only lead to disaster. So she had retreated to Denver where she didn't have to interact directly with him and where her past could still hold her down.

That rationale didn't make as much sense anymore. While she'd succeeded in not seeing him often, she still thought about him every day, found something she wished she could show him or talk about.

Yet she could have taken her career further. If working in the New York office with Ash was too close for comfort, she could have moved to one of the other offices, could have moved into high-level management in one of the other facets of the company. Or left EJ to grow at another firm where the past didn't have a hold on her. Instead, she'd kept playing it safe. Which wasn't safe at all.

"What are you working on?" Ash called over to her desk.

"The Osaka convention. There are twelve meals over the course of the four-day program. It's a barren space so I have a lot of equipment rentals and a temp kitchen. A fair number of people have special diets to accommodate. Some have service animals coming along with them. I've even got a pet pig to deal with."

"Hope that's not what's for lunch."

"Ha. This event is actually turning out to be a toughie. I have speakers, seminar leaders and moderators who aren't in agreement with each other about the programming."

Ash had titanic tasks, as well. Namely, making sure all of their high-level clients whose hands Edward had held for, in some cases, three generations, were a hundred percent comfortable working with Ash now, and that their accounts totaling into the billions were invested and overseen to their satisfaction. The pair of them had dinner over their desks. When they got back to the apartment, Annie was ready to retire to the guest room that had become her home. They'd been at it all day and she could do without yet another evening of them sitting on the couch, barefoot and cozy, drinking tea and munching on cookies while they recapped their progress.

Those evenings had become too wonderful—she'd rather deny herself the pleasure.

In fact, she wasn't able to sleep, replaying Edward's words about being settled and married and what mattered in life. She thought she'd sewn that up tight, stayed in quiet Denver where no one cared about her lack of a romantic life and she simply paid her mortgage every month on her home. Now she'd shaken up her world.

Could she really pull off this hoax, first dating then *breaking up* with her pretend boyfriend? And what if it was followed by taking a position where she'd be working close to him forever?

"Why did you leave the penthouse without me?" Ash grilled Annie, as soon as he got to the office.

"I had a rocky night so I figured I might as well come in early. I didn't want to wake you."

"A-ash." Oh, no. He knew whose voice he'd just heard. Zara burst in like some sort of abstract image of a sunflower, wearing a yellow dress that had sort of fabric petals at the waist, which waived when she walked as if they were in the wind.

He shared a look of frustration with Annie, and she grabbed a stack of papers from the desk and slid past Zara, murmuring, "I'll be right back."

Hey, she was supposed to be shielding him from Zara! So why had she just walked out of the room? He had a million things to do and babysitting Zara was surely not going to be one of them.

"I miss seeing you," Zara cooed as she reached into a yellow tote that matched her dress. She pulled out a fake potted plant, some sort of purple flower, and took it upon herself to place it on Ash's desk. "Just a little reminder of the bloom you and I could still have. How's it going with Annie, anyway?" She gestured with her head at the doorway Annie had just gone through.

"Fine." He looked at the fake plant, looked at Zara's strangely fashioned dress. "My darling," he exclaimed with a theatrical flourish as Annie returned and reclaimed his attention. He rushed over and took the files from her hands, placing them on a nearby table. He wrapped his arms around her, enveloping her completely.

Annie extracted her head from Ash's total

embrace and looked over at Zara. "He's so affectionate."

"Why wouldn't I be, Loviface?" he cooed. That was an endearment he'd just made up. Like Pookie. Was he losing his mind?

Zara squealed, "Loviface?" She hoisted her big tote over her shoulder and stomped out on her yellow high heels, throwing over her shoulder, "Remember what I said, Pookie."

Once Zara had retreated far out of earshot, Ash couldn't help but laugh. Even Annie was giggling. He was sure neither of them wanted to be mean but Zara was *so* over-the-top. He figured someday she'd find a man who would like those very qualities about her that he found so irritating.

"What did she want you to remember, Loviface?" Annie asked, teasingly.

"Some nonsense about how she was still standing by."

"Not on my watch, Loviface."

The next night, Ash tossed the menu from the Chinese restaurant onto the kitchen counter. "I'm tired of eating out of boxes."

"What do you want instead?"

"Let's go do something."

"Where do you want to go?"

"Should we go hear some music? Would you like to go to a jazz club?"

"I'd love to." Sure, out on a date to a club with her rich and attentive boyfriend. There was apparently no limit to how much Ash could feed Annie's fantasies.

He tapped into his phone. "Done. We have a front row table at Wizzy's for ten o'clock." The famous club founded by legendary trumpet player Wizzy Jefferson.

They quickly changed clothes. Annie turned to her new wardrobe and was grateful that the Bergen's purchases had included a tiny sparkly silver dress. She was not used to wearing clothes like that, but clubbing in New York required a certain kind of style. She wasn't used to looking so flashy. It felt a little bit like playacting, but the intention was true. Dressing in front of a mirror, she did love how the dress clung to her shape and shimmied every time she moved.

And she really was ready to step out of her comfort zone, to eclipse the boredom and safety she'd been hiding behind. Strappy sandals completed her nightclub look. A little product in her hair helped lift and zoosh it out, and she was glad to be free of the head-band she wore to keep her hair from looking wild. That was somehow exactly how she did want to look tonight. Going to a New York jazz club in the Village with Ash. She put on some red lipstick.

"Okay." When she stepped out of her side of the penthouse ready to go, Ash made a sound. It was something between a gasp and a moan.

All Annie knew was that it was probably the best sound she'd ever heard.

They stayed at the club for three sets, re-ceiving the first-class treatment, a close-up table with the chairs positioned beside each other to best watch the quartet in action. A stunning singer fronted the group, a woman with gray dreadlocks that cascaded halfway down her back, who used her hands to almost map out the notes she sang. Annie and Ash's shoulders swayed along as they sipped their brandy and she felt relaxed for the first time in a couple of nights.

Tipping home well past midnight, she slipped off her shoes and eased herself down on one of the two reclining chairs that faced out to the night lights of the city, and was glad when Ash followed her lead and sat down on the other one. She had some secrets she was ready to tell him and for some reason after the warmth of the brandy and the vibes of the jazz quartet, she decided this was the moment.

She wasn't going to let him know her big one, the one about the feelings she'd been harboring for a decade, but there were a few things he'd had no knowledge of and she wanted him to. She had the feeling he was keeping something from her, too, and she hoped he'd let it out at some point. It would help her to move forward with her life if everything was out in the open. Maybe then she'd someday be able to let go of him emotionally. And then perhaps this charade and the possible permanent job in New York wouldn't seem like walking on a ground full of minefields. Maybe.

"The city looks spectacular tonight, doesn't it?" she asked in a slow voice.

He nodded. "It does at that."

"Ash, why do you think in ten years we've never really come close to each other again? We've never truly acknowledged what happened at the mentorship."

"We were honest then. The night of the Christmas party was an isolated occurrence.

We knew the other didn't want to take it any further. We left it clean."

"We didn't."

He turned his head toward her which meant she had to do the same and look him in the eye. "What do you mean?"

"There's something I never told you."

He stilled. "What?"

Having sat on the information for so long made it feel heavier than it needed to be. "You were my first, Ash. I was a virgin."

His eyebrows rose as he took that in. "Why didn't you tell me?"

"Because I was afraid then you wouldn't have wanted to be with me."

"You're right," he jumped in. "I wouldn't have! We were drinking! We never talked about birth control. There's some kind of re- sponsibility there."

"For what?"

"I don't know. To make sure you were com- fortable. Or needed anything afterward."

"I wasn't expecting anything. But I wanted you to be my first," she countered. "I'd never talked so honestly as the way we talked to each other. That was really powerful for me. And I knew that it wouldn't last. That we'd go our separate ways. I figured if I could have you as my first, that would be a memory of you I could carry with me for the rest of my life."

He put his hand over his mouth in contemplation then finally said, "Still, I don't like that I didn't know."

"Then when time had passed, I almost thought that I was going to have to tell you. In the end, I didn't."

"That's cryptic. You want to fill me in on what you're talking about?"

She looked out the window, asking the city for courage. Ready to finally tell him.

"The holidays passed and then we were well into the new year. It was a cold winter with dark clouds and icy snow."

"I remember."

"By the end of January, well more than a month had gone by after we had our...moment at the party which was mid-December."

"Yes, that's the math."

"I missed my period."

"You didn't tell me."

"I didn't. I knew you didn't want a relationship and I would have never burdened you with something unplanned that would have changed the whole course of our lives."

"So, what was next?"

"Then I missed the period after that."

"Oh, my gosh."

"Yet I didn't feel pregnant. I had the strong sense that I wasn't pregnant." Which hadn't stopped her from every possible scenario she could conjure. A bouncy baby boy who looked exactly like Ash. Or a cuddly girl in a blanket whose face was a miraculous morph of the two of them. Her walking beside Ash as he pushed a baby stroller through Greenwich Village. Her and Ash and a toddler making sand castles at the beach.

"And?" His voice was full of concern. She needed to quickly put an end to his troubled speculation.

"I was right. I decided to see a doctor to be sure and she said I wasn't pregnant. That it was probably the stress of being in the mentorship and being in New York and that it wasn't uncommon for a young woman to miss a couple of periods. By March I was back on my cycle."

"We had kept a distance from each other by then. But why did you hold all of this from me?"

"Because it might have linked us together.

And neither of us wanted that, right?" She paused. "If there had been a decision to make I didn't want to force you to be any part of it. I didn't want to be a factor that changed your path." Well, she had and she hadn't wanted that at the same time.

That was a lot to say. And she hadn't even told him the biggest bomb. They turned away from each other and both stared out the glass to the skyline again, the skyscrapers even taller than the thirty-ninth floor. Where hopes and dreams grew, some into loss and change, others into adaptation and compromise. Millions of people, millions of stories. Theirs was just one of them.

"I'll see you tomorrow night," Annie said to Ash as she was about to walk out of the office door a few days later. She was flying home to Denver to see her mother and get some more of her clothes and personal items. They'd had that wonderful shopping spree at Bergen's, but now that she was staying in New York to see these events through, she needed more of her own things and to pick up her mail at her house and some paperwork from her office. Yet as silly as it was, she was reluctant to leave Ash even for a short trip.

"Are you sure you don't want me to ride to the airport with you?"

"No, I've seen your calendar. It's chaos today."

He raked his fingers through his hair. His shirtsleeves were rolled up. Annie snuck a long look at the protruding veins in his arms, which for no reason she understood she'd always found profoundly sexy. And wondered for a minute if he still had those tattoos on his chest.

He did get up from his desk to walk her through his office doors. Irene and another couple of PAs happened to be standing there and chatting. Just to fuel the fire, he gave Annie a big hug, and followed it with a warm palm to her cheek. Then capped it off with a kiss that was still safe for the office but far more passionate than it should have been. Annie had no choice but to play-kiss him back, what with people around. In the eyes of the beholders, they were a couple in love.

She spent the flight replaying what had transpired. Playing house with Ash, the ballroom kiss, telling him details about the past she never thought she would. Information he'd been shocked by. Not that any of it mattered now, but she felt some relief in telling him. She hoped she didn't have to tell him more. As she flew across the miles she tried to concentrate on work, event particulars and minutia, to keep her mind from going where it shouldn't, as neither backward nor forward were correct directions.

She returned to New York in a blink, greeted in her guest room by a huge display of multicolored roses on the side table that emitted a delightful fragrance. A note read, "Welcome home." Ash wasn't there when she arrived, which irrationally made her a little bit sad. But they had plans to have dinner with Edward that night.

After opening up her suitcase, she began hanging her clothes. They looked strange in the closet beside the sophisticated ones she'd bought here. Like they belonged to two different women. The drab garments couldn't be the possessions of the same woman who now wore sparkly dresses and body-conscious pieces made of fine fabrics and neutral colors that showed off her curves. And made her feel upwardly mobile. The old clothes belonged to someone who was marching in place, not someone who was ready to move forward, armed with a confident personal style.

Maybe she wasn't as confident as all that yet, but she was on her way. She might not have been a fashionista to rival Ash's usual company, but she was her best self in a way she hadn't been before. Impulsively, she took off her clothes and tried on one of her old dresses, immediately questioning why she'd bothered flying it to New York. A long dress, ankle length and loose fitting. She looked lost inside of it. She pulled out three of her old headbands and hardly remembered ever wearing them. She didn't even know the person in the mirror anymore.

On the plane back she'd allowed herself a little musing on the future. Was the charade really going to come to an end after the gala capped Edward's send-off? Would she go back to Denver and wait for Ash to set up the new position he spoke of? Clearly, he didn't have time to work on that now. Or would she stay in New York, something she was realizing more every day that she wanted. It had been fine seeing her mom and brothers yesterday, but in the short period of time she'd been here, she'd changed, she could feel it in her soul. She wasn't ready to try to explain it to them yet, but she knew it was finally her moment. And she wasn't going to let it pass by.

Annie and Ash walked around the corner from Wall Street as night fell. Even after dark, people still dashed to and fro, and in and out of the mammoth office buildings the area was known for. Deals were made all night long. Work never stopped in this storied district, where the infamous bell at the New York Stock Exchange watched over it all.

Ash darted into a doorway and, after being buzzed in, held the door open for Annie and they entered Club NYNY, a semiprivate restaurant where the elite of the finance industry came to dine. Guests paid an annual fee to become members, which allowed them first crack at available tables for any given date. Some, like Edward, paid a fee high enough to assure him of a favorite table.

"Edward likes it here because he knows everyone. He can have a good meal and relax."

"It's beautiful." Annie surveyed the entrance area.

A tall and wide black onyx reception counter was manned—or was it *womaned*?—by two tall and elegant young women, one pale and dressed in a fitted black dress, the other with dark skin in a purple dress. They looked like statues with their perfect postures and bone structure. One wasted no time with her "Good evening, Mr. Moretti."

"Ladies."

"Follow me, please." The young woman in the purple dress came around the counter and led them toward Edward's table. A formality, as Ash certainly knew where it was.

"Ash, Annie," Edward greeted from the center of the booth, where he had his hand wrapped around a dry martini with two olives. The other two dining companions were to his right.

"Annie, you know Preston Maggis, our COO," Ash said, getting the table reacquainted.

Annie put out her hand to shake his. "It's been a long time since I've seen you in person."

"And you remember our CFO, Rana Haddad," Ash continued.

"Hello, Annie." The two women shook hands.

Edward signaled for Annie to sit at his left in the booth with Ash on her other side. "What would you like to drink?" Ash immediately asked Annie as he knew the waiter would rush over within seconds.

"Same as Mr. Jameson, please."

Edward nodded.

And indeed the waiter, in his tuxedo uniform, had dashed over and heard her order. "Very good. And you, sir?" he asked Ash.

"As well." They settled in against the forest green leather of the booth, the color of which Ash thought emphasized the clubby feel of the place. The same dark green was echoed in the linen napkins, with the white tablecloths flecked with tiny green leaves.

"I've gathered everyone together tonight," Ash began, "to start talking about the VP position I want us to create. With Edward's blessing." He nodded to his mentor.

"Yes."

"I'm sure you know that Annie has been doing a bang-up job for us in Denver for ten years now. I'd like to design the position with, and for, her."

She was radiant in a white dress purchased on their shopping spree. Its neckline was low enough for her delicate collarbones to be on proper display and he had to reel himself in when his mind wandered to what his mouth would feel like on the exposed skin of her dé-colletage, and then upward.

After the kiss in the Empire Ballroom that first night, they'd been diligent about staying away from physical contact other than when they were performing as the loving couple. The private kiss at the ballroom had been a human mistake. Two people who'd had both an emotional and a physical interlude ten years earlier, and who were currently un-attached—it wasn't that surprising that curiosity would draw them to rekindle their chemistry.

He was glad they were mature adults who realized that masquerading as a couple wasn't the same thing as being a couple and that they needed to keep that in the forefront of their minds at all times. The trouble was, that wasn't what was in Ash's heart. In fact, An-nie's smile to Edward just now had been so charming he thought he might melt into one of the little candles in gold votive holders at the table.

Plus, the confession she'd dropped that he had been her first lover was still ricochet-ing through him. He didn't know if he'd ever been with a virgin—except her, apparently.

The women he'd been intimate with presented themselves as sophisticated and he assumed they'd been with other men, but he didn't actually know for certain. He'd always used condoms. He'd never given his encounters much thought, because they hadn't mattered.

Somehow knowing that he was Annie's first was something else entirely. It gave their one night together extra gravity. And that she'd thought it had left her pregnant... He'd hardly been able to get his mind off that.

He was keeping a secret, too, and he knew how much it haunted a person.

"Now, is there anyone else at EJ we need to, in fairness, consider for the position?" Preston injected.

"Fair point," Ash responded. "Annie is by far the most experienced of our event managers. She knows the staff and operations at all of the offices which will be a big plus in working efficiently. I'm bringing her into the creation of the position."

Edward nodded. "I'll handle any questions if the subject is broached. I'm proud of you, Ash."

He was glad to please Edward. Since they'd met, his was always the only vote of confidence Ash had needed, affirmation he'd surely never gotten at home.

"You've accomplished great things and, especially with Annie by your side, you'll take EJ to heights beyond anything I'd imagined. And Annie—" Edward winked "—I'm delighted we're keeping it all in the EJ family both with the new position and with personal matters."

"To EJ," Ash toasted and they lifted their glasses.

The waiter came by to deliver the first course salads served on white plates rimmed with green and silver. Obviously, Edward had taken care of ordering dinner.

"I'm very glad you two have found something with each other."

Annie's eyes drifted away from Edward's at those words. This had to be difficult for her, Ash acknowledged. He'd brought her to New York for her expertise and now, all of a sudden, she was having to navigate the likes of Zara and an Edward who was gleaming nostalgic. Then she'd have to weather Edward's disappointment when they called the relationship off.

Juggling that would be enough, but he was

about to make things even more complicated by asking her to permanently relocate to New York. How they were going to go from pretend lovers, to broken-up, to a professional relationship remained to be seen.

"I wanted Preston and Rana to join us tonight so we can start outlining the scope of the position."

Rana asked, "Annie, tell us how you put an event together. We probably don't know the ins and outs of what it entails."

"Through Edward's generosity we have been producing educational events where we'll invite finance students from a particular university to come for an introduction to a new software, for example."

Ash could tell she was nervous, having to give an impromptu presentation. Her breath hitched and she should have been talking louder. Although this would be a great pitch to Preston and Rana. Ash liked group decisions for EJ—he valued other people's input. He encouraged Annie, "Go on."

"With another of Edward's charities we do big groups of high school students for seminars on the industry as a career choice. We do a whole day or even a weekend of programming. There's the physical space that has to be designed and then what we need to run it. And no matter what we do, we like to feed everyone because that always makes the experience more memorable."

Preston asked, "That's interesting. What are some of the components?"

"Of course we have to lock in a location. I need to know square footage and seating capacity, climate and possible security concerns. There's publicity and invitations and RSVPs. Details about entry and exiting. Presenters, sponsors, speakers, vendors." By the time she got to this point, Annie was fully confident and well-versed in the particulars of her very detailed job. Ash was so proud of her, not that he doubted her for a minute.

In between conversation, they all ate their salads and a waiter bussed away empty plates.

Preston said, "You did a terrific job for us in Los Angeles with the Women Under Twenty-Five weekend."

"Yeah, that one ended up being a challenge because we shared a convention hall with a noisy group and we had to do some emergency soundproofing and reposition our audio and video. Plus, there was a system error at the check-in process so the schedule got backed up."

Rana said, "I've been to dozens of events in my life, but I've never really thought about the work that goes into them."

"That means they were done right."

The entrées were served. Roasted branzino and potatoes with garlic spinach.

Annie continued, "People think it's just about food. That's catering, which is only one facet."

Edward added, "I'm not going to be tottering around once I'm not in the office anymore. I'd like to double our charity efforts. I want to do programming on reentry into employment. For people who take extended time off for parenting or caretaking. I want to see if we can offer something for populations in prisons."

"I think this new position will serve us well."

CHAPTER SEVEN

THE MORNING OF the breakfast was hectic. They hopped into a car in their tracksuits and when they got to the office they'd changed into the pajamas they'd brought, as planned. When Ash stepped out of his private bathroom area, it did take Annie aback. In keeping with the breakfast theme he wore a pair of champagne-colored silk pajamas that were trimmed in black. He looked like he'd stepped out of a black-and-white movie. The pajamas fit his long, lean limbs perfectly. He wore black bedroom slippers. He looked like the financier sophisticate he actually was, but instead of eating cereal standing up at the kitchen counter as he actually did, he seemed like he'd be eating on fine china at a dining table with carved wooden legs while he read every page of the print version of *The New York Times*.

"What?" He must have been reading

something in her face. She probably wasn't covering up the fact that the cosplay of the old-timey pajamas was actually a turn-on to her. Pretty much anything he wore had an effect on her. The sexiest man on Wall Street in his tailor-made suits. The hottest guy in the Village on a casual Sunday in jeans and a leather jacket, drinking an Italian soda at an outdoor café table. Silk pajamas, sure. She had absolutely no objectivity.

"Nothing. You look...great."

He half nodded, not taking in her words. That was okay, they had business to take care of. She'd put on her outfit of a long flannel nightgown in a floral pattern that fell to her ankles. It was like a frontier days style with four buttons leading up to the neckline. Her hair was in a braid and she wore brown lace-up booties. She meant it with a sense of humor. She knew she didn't look alluring like Ash did. They reported to the central conference room of the office where many employees had already begun to congregate.

"Shall I start serving?" the caterer asked Annie.

"Yeah, we'll start with coffee and the mini muffins as everyone is still arriving." She'd decided on coffee, tea and hot chocolate along with three flavors of bite-size muffins—orange cranberry, salted chocolate chip, and chili cheddar.

The tech crew had set up six giant flat-screen monitors surrounding the room so the event could be joined by employees in all of the offices around the globe. They had offices in New York, Dubai, Denver, Rio, Tokyo and New Zealand. All the employees were game to show up at all hours in their themed outfits. From people in sports jerseys and shorts, to silky dressing gowns to terry cloth bathrobes to thick woolen winter socks, everyone got in the spirit of things. Soon, the volume was festive, people arriving and talking to each other from within the same room and others talking to people directly on the screens. In fact, it was as loud as a party could be with laughter and exclamations.

When Edward walked into the conference room, everyone broke into massive applause. He looked like an absolute king in dark blue pajamas topped by a plaid robe. The expression on his face was one of pure delight. After all, this company was his family. The clapping and cheering went on for quite some time. Ash took it all in as well, and Annie knew he was pleased.

"I thank you all, all over the world," Edward said with a sweeping gesture encompassing all of the screens. "EJ is nothing without all of you. I know as Ash leads you into the future, you'll be in good hands."

Breakfast commenced and was rolled out beautifully. Everyone was served an American breakfast of scrambled eggs, slices of thick bacon, pancakes with whipped butter and maple syrup, and sliced bananas with blueberries. Volunteers from each location were asked to say something related to breakfast such as a poem or a joke. Edward sat in the center of the New York conference room enjoying every bit of it.

"My wife has forbidden me from making any more breakfast puns," Aoki in Japan offered. "She says if I do, I'm toast. She just pancake it anymore. How waffle, right? I guess I'm in a jam." He garnered applause.

"Never stay at a haunted B and B," Sergio in Rio warned. "It'll give you the crepes."

There was lots of laughter and fun.

Just as she'd said to the guests at the Club NYNY dinner, a lot of aspects had to work together, and many people congratulated her afterward. Annie had done so many of these events and seen her share of problems. She always kept a close watch and this one worked out great. She was so ready for what Edward spoke of, about expanding their schedule. Getting to the next level. She'd surprised herself by speaking so expertly to the group at dinner. She didn't doubt that Ash's confidence in her had something to do with it.

"I noticed something at the breakfast today," Annie said later that evening when, still in their theme pajamas, she and Ash were crashed out on a sofa, sports on the TV. They lay shoulder to shoulder and thigh to thigh.

"What? I mean other than that Jerry Pomeratz's shorts were so tight I could see his family jewels."

Annie smiled, and having gotten a glimpse of the situation herself couldn't disagree. "No. What I was thinking was…didn't you sort of find a father figure in Edward? When you were younger, didn't that mean something to you, given how you say your own father was so critical?"

"Yeah, without him I doubt I would have succeeded."

"Does his approval make up for what you didn't get from your father?"

"He wasn't m..." Ash stopped abruptly.

"I'm sorry—I hit a nerve."

"No you didn't. It's fine." Only it didn't sound fine. He sounded defensive. She lay her head back on the sofa cushions.

Living with someone was weird, even if the pretending to be a couple only happened outside of the house. Living together was all the moments like this, when real things came to the surface but neither was sure they should be sharing them with another human or keeping them to themselves until they died. All of this, ballroom kisses and jazz clubs and shared private jokes and drinking from the same cup of coffee, moments Annie had spent a decade fantasizing about. The fake version was hard to settle for. Impossible, as a matter of fact.

"What did you think of the food today?" She decided changing the subject was the path of least resistance.

"Good. The pancakes held up well."

She didn't know what to say next. "Gandielle in New Zealand was hilarious with her good-night dance she said she and her sisters used to do."

"And the whole American contingent seemed to agree that milk and cookies were the all-time best bedtime snack."

"I do so many breakfast events I feel like I know what people eat everywhere in the world for their first meal of the day."

"Did you eat a family breakfast growing up?"

Annie gulped. Now it was her turn to react to an innocent question. "Breakfast—" she grimaced and then blew some breath from her cheeks "—was kind of a nightmare at my house." The floral flannel nightgown she'd worn for the event today and was still in, a little girl's nightclothes, only added to the painful memories. "We would wake up wondering whether my dad made it home that night."

"Hmm," Ash grumbled in a low voice. "That's rough."

No one, except maybe her brothers would understand the shame that made her feel. That her first thoughts of the day weren't whether she was going to pass her math test or go to someone's birthday party that weekend. No, at the Butterfield house it was the fear and dread of roll call.

"If he was home, he'd be asleep. We'd report to each other as to whether we remembered saying good-night to him the night before, on the rare occasion he'd stayed in for the evening. If he was home in the morning, he would maybe stumble into the kitchen to pour half a cup of coffee into a mug and drink it straight down, black, and then likely tell my mother that it was either too strong, too weak, too hot or too cold. There was no chance he could just drink it down without an insult to her."

"I'm sorry you had to witness that." Ash instinctively laid his hand over her wrist, running his thumb back and forth on her skin in a gesture of such tenderness, she couldn't believe it was happening. Why was she telling him all of this in such detail? She could have just given short, clipped responses like he did when she'd pried about Edward being a father figure to him. In any case, the feeling of the pad of his thumb rhythmically moving to soothe her was maybe the sort of thing real lovers did. She wouldn't know for sure, as she'd never had intimate times like this. Yet she wanted him to continue.

"We'd know if he hadn't come home because we had to pass by their bedroom on the way to the kitchen. If that was the case, the bed would already be made. Maybe my mom didn't want us to see a bed where one side of the blanket was rumpled and the pillow had dents with the other side of the bed military tight, pillow in place, clearly never slept on." She knew that her mom felt as much shame as her children did at that unhappy illustration of the family home. "She'd make silly talk about school projects or what she packed in our lunches, trying to divert us from the big ball of air my dad's absence seemed to waft through the house. And we had to pretend it was normal, that it was one of those mornings and it was no big deal. Like it was the same at any other family's breakfast table."

Silence thickened the air. In fact, Annie felt hot and wanted to tear the heavy nightgown off her body. But there was nowhere to go. Ash's thumb never stopped its caress; she knew she needed to just lie there and accept its comfort. She bit back tears because those recollections had always dictated her life.

They were the reason she was here with Ash now. Why making love with him ten Christmases ago and why kissing him at the Empire Ballroom a couple of weeks ago could never have been the starts to relationships filled with security and trust. That, she'd never have. She'd have to settle for the beautiful pad of Ash's thumb commiserating with her, consoling her, understanding her like no one else had.

And that wasn't too bad. It was so much better than nothing.

After a long period of quiet on the couch, Annie spoke again. Ash knew she was lost in emotions she was trying to process. Sitting together and talking, debriefing after the breakfast, had become the type of ritual he could imagine doing for the rest of his life.

She was welcome to weep, rage, divulge or do whatever she wanted. He was grateful to hear it.

"So," she finally said aloud when she'd presumably collected herself. "What about you? Let's hear your dirty laundry. What was breakfast like at the Moretti household in New Jersey?"

He winced at the way she said the Moretti household, as that had taken on new meaning than the one it had had when he was a child. "A shit show, just like your house. Most every morning he found something to be pissed off at me about."

"*He* being your father?"

Ash inhaled deeply. "Karl. He'd ask about schoolwork and if I had anything but top marks, which I often actually did have, he'd tell me what a good-for-nothing I was. Or if heaven forbid I left a sock in the bathroom or something like that. He'd barrel into the kitchen and slap my face or the side of my head, screaming about the whole house being out of control."

"Oh my gosh, Ash. Didn't your mother stick up for you or try to at least stop him from hurting you?"

"No. She stayed out of it. I think they'd decided between the two of them from the beginning that he was going to be the father he'd be, and she wasn't going to rock the boat. Warm and fuzzy and loving wasn't going to be our family."

"Did he ever hit her?"

"Not in front of me. I don't know what went

on between the two of them behind closed doors." Yes, he did. He wanted to tell Annie the unspeakable. It was about to come out of his mouth. It might help him to tell another living soul rather than to keep it bottled up inside forever. Maybe he could finally grow past it. Annie was the only person he'd ever wanted to tell. "I know now that they kept a secret between them. There was always a bond that I wasn't part of."

By now, Annie had turned to face him. Her lips pursed. "What kind of secret, Ash? What do you mean?"

Shame and hurt and anger released from every pore in his body all at once.

The moment was happening, whether Ash was ready for it or not.

"Karl Moretti wasn't my father."

"What?" Wide-eyed shock took over her face.

"I didn't know it at the time. My mother doesn't know who my real father is." The truth echoed between his ears. "She was with a few different guys at the time. One she met in a bar and never got his phone number. Another who didn't even live in New Jersey. Another, a married man. And then she met Karl at a party."

"She never found out who got her pregnant?"

"No. When she told Karl she was pregnant, he offered to marry her. He said he'd raise her child as his own as long as she never told anyone."

Ash practically swallowed his own throat. Yes, his mother had agreed never to tell anyone. Not even her own son. Not even telling her own child that his father might not have been his father.

"So if he agreed to raise you, why did he treat you so badly?" Annie pressed with a logical question.

"Because he couldn't go through with it. I always wondered why I didn't look anything like him. He had curly blond hair, and was short and thick. My mom was fair. I have dark hair and eyes. I don't look like either of them."

"And that mattered?"

"It did to him—a constant reminder that I probably wasn't his. And he couldn't stand it. He'd told my mother he'd raise me as his, but when it played out, he couldn't. He hated me for it. And showed me that hate every day of his life."

"I'm so sorry. Did your mother finally tell you?"

Ash was numbed by his own words, breathing heavily. "After he died, I did one of those mail-away DNA tests. That's how I found out my ancestry was nothing like his. When I confronted my mom, she didn't deny it but still maintained that she didn't know who my true father was. That she'd thought all along that me not knowing might help Karl love me more."

It made Ash almost nauseated to think about it. As was often the case, his mother came from a family with a history of domestic violence. Ash's grandmother had been a tiny slip of a woman, who whispered into a room unnoticed, so practiced had she become at not trying to draw attention, not to stir any simmering pots.

"Do you have contact with your mom?"

"Once in a while. I pay for her to live in Florida in a senior community. I pay her medical bills and fly down there a couple of times a year. We have nothing positive to reminisce about so it's superficial chitchat about what she had for dinner or a TV show she watched. I think she plays cards with other people there, so she keeps busy. I'm sure she works to block out the past, too."

Coming clean had been scary, yet the secret had taken over and decided for itself to leap out of his mouth. Would his life be different now? Would he be somehow healed of something? He knew it wasn't like that; people weren't suddenly changed. Yet as he spewed all of the bile and junk he held inside, he did feel a metamorphosis, that he was letting go of a cocoon he didn't need anymore.

Wow. He'd told someone. He slumped forward, shell-shocked.

The quiet between them lasted long enough to become uncomfortable.

Annie finally broke the stalemate, for which Ash was grateful. "We've both held a lot inside."

He turned to her, needed to see her face as they sat on the couch in his lonely man's palace. His hands reached for the sides of her soft face, bringing his lips to hers. And, in what felt as pure and natural as sunrise, she lifted her arms around his shoulders, her hands gliding along to the back of his neck and then down across his shoulder blades. He couldn't believe the loveliness of her touch, of her nimble fingertips. They were no longer those kids in the cubicle at Christmas, hungry and maybe even a little wild. They touched like adults now, with gravitas, both longing for a communication that went far beyond words.

"Annie." There, he'd said her name, as if to confirm that finally, finally, he let someone see his authentic self.

His palms moved slowly down the lovely column of her neck, his fingers slipping under the flannel of the silly nightgown she'd worn for the breakfast that seemed a hundred days ago. His hands touched her delicate collarbones, utilizing all ten of his fingers in a sensual pleasure he took his time with.

If their lips swayed elsewhere, each soon returned to the other's. So absorbing were their kisses that it was as if each of them was taking the other further and still further away from brutal truths and into a hidden paradise. Holding each other's burdens, melding into each other.

His began to undo the little placket of pearly buttons on her nightgown, as the neckline was preventing him from the further exploration his hands were destined for. They were tightly sewn and it wasn't without struggle—one, two, three, four and finally the two sides of the garment flapped open and he could kiss her throat the way he wanted to, with a thousand teeny tiny taps, urging himself to go slower and slower. She let out a little moan of pleasure that arrived as a vibration inside of her that met his lips, and the thrill stirred his body so low that his own moan of pleasure met hers.

CHAPTER EIGHT

A DREAM ANNIE had been living in for ten years was coming true. Ash's hands were on her. She had a moment of private embarrassment reminding herself of just how many times she'd lain in bed in her house in Denver with eyes tightly shut imagining this with him. To be with him again but this time as adults. He'd never known, and still didn't, how much he'd colored the last decade for her. How nobody had ever matched up to him. How even Jack had been a shoddy substitute.

"Can I take you to bed?" Ash murmured, his sultry voice spreading sexy words over her like a swath of warmth.

"Yes, I want that." So much.

"I do, too."

He got up off the couch and extended a hand to help her up, as well. Then, without letting go, he led her to his side of the penthouse, the master suite where she hadn't spent time since she'd been staying here, her mind turning it into a mysterious sanctuary she wasn't part of. As they passed the bar counter, he grabbed a bottle of water and two glasses, his other hand still firmly holding hers.

They moved through his private sitting area—a small sofa, a desk, and a couple of big comfy chairs with side tables, all positioned to take in yet another city view and the large flat-screen TV on one wall. Underfoot was padded carpeting, in contrast to the fine wood of the living room floors. "Nice digs," she smiled.

"Not bad, huh."

She peeked to one side as they passed his dressing area and then to the other to check out his lavish bathroom. In the main chamber of the room, he placed the water and glasses on a table. She followed his movements and had a moment's panic when she caught sight of his bed. Luxe café au lait–colored linens, duvet and a dozen lush pillows invited her. The words came out of her mouth before she could decide if saying them was a good idea. "What are we doing?" In the back recesses of her mind were the kisses at the ballroom and their vow to keep fake things fake.

His first answer came via a slow and silent caress down her back, so slow in fact that it was a titillated agony waiting for him to land at the small swerve below her waist. She wanted to slip that heavy nightgown off but her head was swirling. Would this be smart for her, heart and soul? The kiss at the ballroom had been a little slip, but this would be something different entirely. Even though it was what she wanted, could she live with it possibly meaning nothing, merely creating another memory to harbor? Or maybe it would be a way for her to finally let go. Of him. Wasn't that what she needed if she was going to work with, but not love, him in the future? One time with him as an adult. As completion of a cycle.

His second answer came. "We don't have to if you don't want to."

Of course, he'd say that, he was a gentleman after all. He wasn't going to do anything against her will.

"After we accidentally kissed in the ballroom…"

He interrupted, "Do people accidentally kiss?"

"That's true," she laughed.

He kissed her on the mouth again, filling her like a well that had been empty from drought. "I know that we're not relationship types and that we're playing a game at the office. But I can't help myself from wanting you. I just can't help it."

It might be a risk to her heart, but she wasn't going to turn this moment down. Having him for a short time that was supposed to be fake was better than not having him ever at all. She could handle it. Once. The marriage ruse would end. As they agreed, Annie would appear to be the one to break it off with public promises that they'd remain friends and support each other in their future romances and endeavors.

Then, Ash and his execs would create this new vice president position and Annie would take it, presumably move to New York and work with him every day. It was all for the good of EJ, for the team. She'd rise to it, the task of seeing him every day but having nothing personal between them. See him date women who meant nothing to him. Or she wouldn't be able to, and she'd insist they headquarter the position in Dubai, after all, her reason kept a secret.

She deserved this one night. After years and years of loyalty, letting him occupy her thoughts and feelings. She could afford this one night to re-up the memories that were going to have to keep her for a lifetime. In fact, tonight he'd told her the deepest reason why he wouldn't be hers forever. How horrible for him, to find out the man who was a terrible father to him wasn't even his real father. And to double down on the hurt, that his mother knew the truth behind his father's hatred but hadn't told him. And then, in typical Ash fashion, he still supported his mother financially when he'd have every right to turn his back.

She knew that his revelation to her had brought up enormous emotion. And that he was reacting to that, morphing it into desire. She also knew that it wasn't as simple as that; it wasn't as if he'd reach for any woman in passing to bury his sorrow. She knew him better than that. He wanted this reconnection as much as she did.

Ash brought her to his bed and laid her

down as if she was fragile and precious. His might took her over as he climbed on top of her. It was exquisite, his height and weight on her, around her. Her hands caressed anything they could reach, his shoulders, the planes of his chest muscles, his sinewy upper arms.

He took her face in his hands as he captured her mouth, holding it steady as he kissed her again and again. And the more he kissed her, the more she wanted him to. Looking at his face, his history in his eyes, the slope of his nose and the cut of his jaw. Him pressing into her. She could feel his arousal as he undulated on top of her with each kiss. His hardness driving her with passion, ready to open her sexuality like an envelope. His masculinity was rigid and charging, trapping her in the most wonderful way.

He backed off and in one swoop removed the nightgown she was so ready to shed. He shrugged off his pajamas in a quick motion and promised to be right back while he retrieved a condom. Quickly, he was naked, protected and on top of her. She hugged him tightly, not wanting to let a sliver of gap between them. She opened her legs, an instinctive signal to him that she was ready. With no time wasted he took hold of her hips and inched into her, until he couldn't enter any further. He took her deeply, with circular grooves, and her hips rose and fell to find him each time. In moments, if there'd been any elegance it was stripped away. There was nothing gentle, they were broken and hurting and needy and desperate for each other. Just as she'd always been. The poignancy of thirty-two turned out to be not that different from twenty-two, after all. They were both world-rocking encounters.

Annie awoke to morning in Ash's bed. Gazing around at the simple but tasteful furniture upholstered in brown and black, and the soothing nature paintings on the wall, she may as well have been at a hotel for the lack of familiarity. She'd only known her guest quarters in his large apartment. This was most certainly her first night in the bed so big it must have been custom made. One thing that was familiar, though, was the man lying on his side facing her, as if he was waiting for her to wake up.

"Good morning," she cooed with a stretch like a cat.

"And you." He placed a feather of a kiss on her cheek.

She was completely naked under the high thread count of his sheets, and assumed he was as well since he was bare from the waist up. In the light of day she was able to finally spy what she'd speculated on. Whether or not he still had those tattoos on his chest that he'd had ten years ago. Answered. They were still there. She'd wondered if in his success, he'd had them removed, given that they had such an amateur look to them, random on his chest. They were nothing like the living art some people wore, vividly colored flowers or portraits of loved ones or the intricately drawn shadowy gray styles she'd seen. His were here and there, too small, with no relation to each other, in unmatched blueish and black ink that looked random.

It was when she'd first met him at that mentorship retreat that she'd seen them. He'd quickly changed shirts to go for a hike. They had caught her eye with fascination, as anyone's that were usually hidden under the wraps of their clothes would. But she'd hidden her surprise at their ugliness. During that fateful night of frenzy at the holiday party, clothes hadn't been removed. She hadn't known how to get the conversation started about them back then. She didn't know now either, but curiosity was gnawing at her.

"I kind of remember your tattoos from when we went to that retreat." She leaned over to kiss one in the center of his solar plexus, what looked to be a thin rendering of a bird in flight, its wingspan the focus. As soon as she'd said that she was sorry—she didn't really want him to know that she'd spent a decade contemplating the nuances of his body.

"You do?" See, he thought that was strange.

She craned up to kiss the Chinese symbol inked on his left pectoral muscle, loving the feel of her mouth on him. "How many tattoos do you have?"

"Five." All of them were confined to the front of his torso. None reached to his shoulder or arms, and therefore would always be hidden by a shirt, something she assumed was on purpose.

"Do they all have certain meaning for you?" Although it was an assumption, she asked it as a question. Then she arched up to kiss his mouth again, softening, making sure this didn't become an interrogation.

"The Chinese symbol's meaning is morality." It wasn't hard to figure out why he'd chosen that one.

Her fingers tapped to the side of his ribs where the next one was a crude drawing like from a children's picture book. It was a small home. On fire. Flames lashed out from the windows, one on each side of the open front door.

"A home on fire. Your childhood."

"Yeah. I got that one on my eighteenth birthday, the day I moved out of my house."

"The front door of the house is open."

"So I could escape."

"Same with the bird?"

"That was my first one. I was only sixteen when a friend of mine did it in his bathroom with a needle dipped in ink. I kept it from my dad, er, from Karl, for as long as I could because I knew he'd be pissed off. He beat the crap out of me when he finally saw it."

Annie bit her lip at what he'd been through. "Ash."

"Screw him, though. That bird meant flight."

Next she ran her finger across the starburst on his hip bone.

"I got that one when I was twenty-one and graduated college. I guess it meant hope."

"Were your parents, your mom and Karl, at your graduation?"

"She was there. He didn't come. Were your parents at yours?"

"Yeah. They sat separately. My mom sat with my brothers and my dad sat alone. Lots of people's families went out to eat and celebrate after. We didn't. My mom and brothers and I went home to a store-bought cake. I don't know what my dad did but he didn't come right home."

"Sorry."

Feeling the bird again, Annie wanted to get back to the topic of Ash's tattoos, tired of her own story. This was fascinating, his impulse to mark his experiences on his body. To have them forever, his album, his gallery, his scrapbook. "Do you mind me asking about them?" He looked at her with all the grief in the world on his face. And then flipped a switch. He leaned back and crossed his hands behind his head so she could gander to her heart's content.

She pointed to the last one below his right rib cage. "An anchor. I celebrated getting accepted into Edward's mentorship program. That one was right before I met you."

"Thank you for sharing all of that with me."

"Thank you for being interested."

Ash stepped into his well-designed shower in his master bathroom. The clear glass doors and their brushed-nickel handles opened to a huge shower with a bench inside. There was a multi-setting showerhead unit. One notch offered a rain shower while another produced a forceful spray with six or so settings, from pulsing massage to a strong jet.

He chose a hot temperature and immersed his body under it. As water cascaded down his face and his hair, he closed his eyes. There was a lot to process.

Namely, Annie. What they'd done last night took their pretend relationship to a height he'd certainly not been counting on. To think, all he'd been trying to do was get Zara away from him in a way that wouldn't be detrimental to Edward. He should have known better. Even though so much time had passed since he and Annie had their Christmas fling long ago, he'd always kept his eye on her from afar. She'd been the wrong person to dally with.

Last night they'd truly reunited with the spilling out of those confidences they'd both figured on holding quiet.

He lathered himself with the foamy musk-scented soap he favored. Indeed, he'd come a long way from being yelled at and berated for using too much soap. He swirled the bar all over his chest and under his arms, down between his legs, using his hand to scrub himself all over. He relived Annie's small hands on his body. Exquisite. He then set the strongest water tap to pound down on him until he was fresh and clean. After drying himself as thoroughly as he'd washed, once satisfied he wrapped the towel around him and tucked it below his waist.

Moving to the large bronze-framed mirror above the sink, he faced his reflection and just stood there for a moment. He felt transformed in a way he couldn't put his finger on. It was Annie. She made everything different. She stripped everything down, shed a light on the fact that despite all the fancy soap and the ridiculously super-sized apartments in the world, he was a damaged man living half a life that cheated him out of all he could have.

He studied his chest in the mirror, something he hadn't done in a long while. Annie had been so fascinated by his tattoos. No one had ever asked about them before. Now that he thought about it, there was no one to really notice them. The kind of interludes he had with women usually took place in the dark and ended before dawn, not because he had any particular aversion to nudity, simply because he went from hotel rooms in the dark of night to early escapes that avoided the awkwardness of breakfast with someone he was never going to see again.

As he stared at those five markings in the mirror, there was no question that they were grotesque. That was just what he liked about them. Raw. They were badges of honor, survivor's medals. The proof that he'd gotten out, knowing full well how many didn't. Those misshapen, messy, unartistic markings were his witnesses.

There was something frighteningly meaningful that Annie was the one to ask about them. With her, he seemed to want to be as naked as possible. Yes, he wanted her to ask about the tattoos, his little symbolic scars. He'd loved, *loved*, when she touched each one of them as he told their tales. They'd come to life, inviting her into their stories, their proverbs, their sermons. As she'd worked her way to kissing each one, her breath on his skin had been a salve, making each carry more sensation than the unaltered skin that surrounded them did.

He could imagine having brought her into the shower with him instead of letting her go off to start the coffee and toast. He'd lather her the way he'd soaped up himself, not missing an inch, and how he'd have enjoyed using one of the handheld spouts to wash her clean.

He could bask in their nudity, proud of it, proud that they could both show their gunshot wounds to the world, proving that they'd prevailed. He could see them running naked through a meadow of tall grass and tiny flowers. He could see them skipping into the ocean, never letting go of each other's hand. Or in a pristine swimming pool, diving to touch the mosaic of the bottom and then springing their way back up. Naked under a waterfall, the intensity of the gushing water cascading down on them. Standing on a coastal hill like lighthouses, beacons in a stormy night. Or floating on a cloud, reclining in the puffy cotton, laughing. Or on a Manhattan rooftop, syncing their own movements, him on top of her, falling into her center, the population of eight million disappearing as there would be only them.

Should he take Edward's advice, that coupling completed a life in a way that nothing else did? Something the older man himself had missed out on until the very end. Something Ash had assumed wouldn't be on his path. Yes, he could be hurt, betrayed, lied to, endure loss more destructive than any he'd already known, but...

One more look at his tattoos. Tomorrow night, they'd be covered in a Saville Row suit for the theater performance. Then under a crisp apron at the pasta-making party. And by a designer tuxedo at the gala. Annie knew what was under all of his guises. The real him, the kid who had to suck up the injustices foisted upon him and the professional who'd learned how to mask.

Did he have to put himself in danger? Annie was the only one it would be worthwhile for, a knowledge that had been foggy in front of him and only now could he suddenly see it. Some sort of destiny had brought her back to his life, to his front door. Could he take the risk of letting her in? Could he believe she wouldn't explode what was left of his heart?

At the office, they worked for hours on the auction for the gala. Annie took a conference call with the Hotel Fifth management and went over some details on the schedule of the evening. They both received what seemed like endless texts, phone calls and emails.

"Glad we could count on you, Mrs. Deon," Ash said, finishing up a call to a longtime client family who had donated a week at their beach house on Cape Cod.

Annie had to admit that every time she looked over to see him diligently working, it brought a secret smile to her face that she kept tiny. She'd been well aware that, after years, it wasn't healthy for her to still be glorifying him, even though she couldn't seem to help herself, given that something he'd say or a facial expression during a video conference would be enough to set her daydreams off again. Other than Jack and a few unsatisfying one-nighters with friends of friends of friends she'd met at a party or wedding, she'd had nothing else going on the romantic front. She'd convinced herself that still wishing for Ash was harmless. Way down deep, she knew it wasn't.

The irony was that being with him was infinitely better than anything she'd ever envisioned. The real Ash, such an explosive yet attentive lover, perceptive while fierce.

He looked over. "Did we eat?"

She laughed. "We had a late breakfast of coffee, coffee, coffee and yogurt."

"Let's get out of here for a while, we need a break." He buzzed into his intercom. "Irene, can you grab us a couple of sweaters?" Irene kept a small wardrobe in a storage room to accommodate whatever spontaneous need arose.

"I thought we'd just grab a sandwich at the café downstairs?" Annie quizzed.

"Why don't we do a little better than that?"

"What will that be?"

"I want to be on water." As they left the office, Irene handed Ash two white cable-knit fisherman's sweaters as if she had read Ash's mind.

He pressed the button for the elevator and tapped into his phone. Outside the building's lobby, a driver pulled up and Ash opened the passenger door for Annie to slide in. She moved over so that he could join her and he instructed the driver to take them to the pier. Then, after arriving at their destinations, he quickly escorted Annie out of the car and led her to the dock that was indicated on his phone.

"Is this yours?" she asked as he took her by the hand and they crossed the gangway onto the dock to the boat.

"No, I don't own a boat. I just rented it for us for a few hours."

"Just like that?"

He raised his eyebrows and shrugged. "Just like that." She smiled.

"I'm Laritza, welcome aboard *Old Pals*." As they stepped onto the ironically named boat they were greeted by a fortyish woman who wore a white shirt tucked into white pants and a traditional captain's hat. "I'm your captain for our ride."

"Very good, thank you. I ordered some food, did it arrive?"

"Yes, sir. I'll be serving you as soon as we get away from shore. May I offer you a glass of wine or water to start?"

"Sparkling water would be great. Annie?"

"Yes, thanks."

He guided her to sit on the U-shaped booth that was covered in cushions of sailcloth, white and blue striped. The bench was so comfortably deep that they could lie back as if they were propped up on a bed. When Laritza brought their water, she folded up a couple of panels that created a table for each of them with wells to hold drinks so that they wouldn't spill should there be any rough seas.

"Do you want a sweater?" Ash offered Annie and she took one, pulling it over the silk T-shirt that had become one of her chic businesswoman pieces. It was huge on her petite frame and she pushed up the sleeves to above her wrists. With that, the captain coaxed them out of the pier and onto the Hudson River.

"Where are we going?"

"Just a tour around the island. Did you ever go anywhere when you were a kid?"

She wrapped her hand around the water glass and took a sip. "Certainly not. My father was gone for days on end, no doubt taking women here and there. We never found out the specifics. Sometimes he'd come home with a suntan. My brothers and I were always left with our mom." She recoiled at the memory of the front door to their house with its chipped eggshell paint. Of hours spent waiting to see if her father was going to come home from work on any given night. Not that it much mattered, as he had never been interested in anything his kids had to say. He had always been a disappointment to her, better in fantasy than in person. "When I came to New York for the mentorship, that was the first time I'd been away from home. Didn't I tell you that then?"

"That, I don't remember. What about later?"

"I take my allotted vacations from EJ. I have a friend in California I visit. She and her husband have a small winery. It's lovely there." He didn't know anything about her life in Denver, her friends, her pastimes. She wondered if he'd ever thought about it, if and what he'd thought about her.

"I assume you've traveled to the EJ offices and seen what the other regional events managers are up to?"

Captain Laritza wheeled over a cart. She served them utensils wrapped in heavy cloth napkins. "Cold steamed lobster, vegetable crudités, and chocolate mousse for dessert."

"Thank you. Annie, is there anything else you'd like?"

"This looks fabulous."

The captain returned to the wheel. Indeed, the big chunks of simply prepared lobster with a squeeze of fresh lemon did taste good on first bite.

"Yeah." She sat back in her seat and brought the plate to her lap so she could pick chunks from it as they talked. "I've been to all of the EJ offices at one point or another. I love the lobby in Dubai."

"Yes, with that reflective fountain and the narrow glass windows." Funny that they'd both visited at separate times, had never been there together.

What a sight it was to watch the sea breeze tousle Ash's hair while he bit a succulent piece of shellfish, sexy as could be in his sunglasses and the thick white sweater.

What would really come to pass after the gala? She'd used her mother and brothers as an excuse for staying in Denver, but she didn't need them and they didn't need her. They were each other's testimony, but it was their very shared experience that would forever keep them at a distance from each other. She'd hidden in Denver.

Her self-protection told her that while Ash had his place as a brush with a lifelong fantasy, she'd better not count on more. He'd been clear he had nothing to give. Neither did she. Yet she couldn't stop musing about the possibility that gashes could heal and even scars could fade. Winner could take all.

"What about you? Did you travel at all when you were a kid?" She came back to the conversation. She was with him in the here and now, and would be present for every minute of it, even if it was only temporary.

"No. Karl couldn't keep a job for very long so he never had any vacation time. He wasn't exactly concerned with showing my mom and me a good time." Enough said, those words flew out to the sea air for a bit while they ate their delicious lunch. After listening to the sound of the waves Ash finally asked, "What did you wish for when you were a kid?"

"The obvious. To live in a family where the parents loved each other. I'd wish that they would talk to each other, kiss when one of them got home, you know, like on TV."

Ash let out a belly laugh. "Like on TV.

That's a real laugh-or-cry statement. I hate TV. It makes kids have expectations."

"I agree." She nodded emphatically, and then leaned over to kiss him, a soulful kiss like lovers shared. It filled her up, made her feel as fresh as the air she was breathing and the brace of the water they sailed on.

They both stood and moved to the brass railing on deck so they could enjoy the sights.

"There's the Empire State Building," Annie said, pointing. "I read that was the tallest building in the world until nineteen seventy-two."

"The Chrysler Building has always been my favorite. See those gargoyles and car ornaments with the spire. You can tell it's to represent an automobile manufacturer."

As the captain took them farther down the Hudson, it seemed both natural and extraordinary and, strangely, a combination of them both. She'd known him for so long yet she didn't know little things like his favorite building or whether his family took vacations. How far would they go learning about one another beyond the scope of work?

As they approached the Statue of Liberty, the gift from France stood tall and magnificent and fearless as she always had, a symbol of freedom and hope since 1886. Annie hadn't seen it in a while. The captain got them as close to Liberty Island as was possible so they could take in the majestic scale of Lady Liberty.

"Ash, like in the poem, are we the huddled masses yearning to breathe free? The wretched refuse of your teeming shore?"

CHAPTER NINE

"NICE TO SEE you again, Mr. Colon." Ash shook yet another hand as guests filtered up to the Castle Theatre's mezzanine for the party. He surrounded Mrs. Colon's bony hand with both of his. "You look lovely, as always. I'd like for you to meet tonight's hostess, Annie Butterfield. She's been with EJ for ten years but we've been hiding her in Denver." Annie shook both of their hands.

"*It's going to be our night*," sang the performer who was walking around accompanied by a saxophone player during what was the cocktail hour. It was a famous Broadway tune. The sound of the horn echoed the melody. "*Everything feels so right. We're setting this town alight. Full of will, grit and might.*"

"Mr. Baum and Mr. Adebesi." Ash shook the hands of another couple of clients. "This is Annie Butterfield, our event manager and my girlfriend. Let's get you a drink." She wasn't even sure at this point if he should be introducing her as his girlfriend given that the events would be completed by the end of the week, and it had been agreed that the charade would end and they'd announced their breakup. Although that now seemed like the last thing in the world she wanted to see happen.

The mezzanine was filling up. Ash was being properly welcoming. She knew it didn't come naturally to him to schmooze, obviously someone with his upbringing wasn't likely to be overtly social, but he'd taught himself how over the years and now he was good at it. It was a necessary part of the job and would be even more so when he became CEO.

"We will come take a bite. We are ready for flight. We will fly like a kite. Now our future is bright." The singer continued to belt out with the saxophonist wailing as they wove through the crowd, gaining everyone's attention.

"That was genius," Ash said to Annie when finally they were able to stand together and watch the proceedings from a corner. "Having the singer snake around the crowd. Setting the tone for the evening."

"Everyone seems to be enjoying it. Here

come the charcuterie cups." She pointed to several waiters who held trays with dozens of little clear cups. "I worked with the caterer to get away from the same old boring hors d'oeuvres at every party. Although we'll actually serve some classics at the gala just for tradition's sake."

"Crispy fried things." Ash crossed his fingers to make her smile. Which prompted a slow grin from her. She'd give a big squishy kiss to her boyfriend except that she didn't want to smear her makeup.

"The cups each hold candied walnuts and dark chocolate-covered blueberries on the bottom, topped with a stick of cheese, a pick that holds olives, another with baby tomatoes, and a seeded breadstick."

"You're making my mouth water." It wouldn't look right for the CEO to be chomping while his guests were arriving. "Promise you'll save us some to have at home tonight." *Home.* The more he said that word the more she liked hearing it, his tastefully solitary room in the sky had started to seem like a real home.

She glanced over to Edward, who was toasting a drink with a couple of older men she recognized from his club. He appeared to be having a wonderful time. It was good to see him enjoying himself after losing Betty. It had made him so happy to hear that Ash and Annie were a couple—that was something he had so wanted for Ash. It would be hard on him when they broke up from their masquerade.

Ash jutted his chin toward Preston and Rana, the COO and CFO respectively who'd been at dinner the other night. "You dazzled the heck out of them."

"That's good news. I definitely pulled out all the stops to show off how much I knew."

"You're sure not boring Denver Annie when you don't want to be."

She giggled. "I guess my time has come."

Edward spoke of love and valued love, yet romantic love had eluded him for far too long. What if Ash opened himself to loving Annie and then he lost her? Having Annie and then losing her would be too much to bear.

Zara was in attendance tonight. Ash saw her texting into her phone. She was dressed over-the-top as always in a Goth-y outfit of black and green, lacy and overdone. His mind hadn't been on her at all, other than as the catalyst for the pretend romance that felt decidedly not like pretend. She spotted him and began walking over, not noticing at first that he was with Annie. When she did, she quickly pivoted in a different direction toward someone she knew.

As Zara walked away, Ash took notice of couples in the room. The Colons, who were now seated at one of the mezzanine banquettes. He knew that they had gotten married when they were very young and had kids who themselves yielded a handful of grandchildren. What had their path to a long marriage been? Did they have to overcome hurt and fear?

Then he spotted Franklin and Emily Chew, who came to the United States from China without a penny and made themselves into billionaires with frozen food products based on old family recipes. Had their union been a smooth ride, or had they had obstacles to face before they could commit to a life together as a couple, as partners, as friends?

Somehow those two couples had found their way through the destructive forces that no doubt had worked to keep them apart. Might Ash and Annie be able to do the same?

Lifelong unions required faith. Not one of his strong suits.

There was Rhys Tyson and his new wife. Ash believed it was his third. What demons had kept Rhys from making a marriage pact that stuck? A dysfunctional childhood? Didn't everyone have barriers, skeletons? It would be so easy to make a fatal mistake. He'd recently been to Iron Strauss and Billy McClintock's wedding. Would they need to unpack any emotional baggage and leave it behind in order to sustain a love, a home, maybe a family? Would they be able to?

Ash wanted to think he could, but he still didn't really believe it.

After the cocktail hour, the guests were invited to file into the theater for the command performance of *We Found Home*. Inside the auditorium red velvet ropes closed off the back rows so that the select group of two hundred guests could sit together front and center to create a unified experience rather than sitting willy-nilly anywhere in the fifteen-hundred-seat capacity theater.

The auditorium had a magnificent ceiling. A large circle of bronze sunbursts from the center encircled a frosted glass and bronze chandelier. Organ chambers stood on the side of the stage, and a proscenium arch with

Egyptian flowers in bronze adorned the top
and sides.

The houselights dimmed to half and a few
chimes encouraged guests to take their seats
for the performance. Once everyone was in
place, Annie and Ash sat in the last row of
the designated area, her on the end so she
could be easily accessible if she was needed,
and could be called out without disturbing the
rest of the guests.

The lights dimmed fully, the curtain rose
up in a slow and graceful swath and the music
started. The private performance began. The
guests were clearly excited about this special experience because they applauded and
cheered as loudly as if the theater had been
sold out with patrons.

A hit for over a year and the winner of
several Tony awards, *We Found Home* was
a high-energy show with the kind of preci-
sion singing and dancing and orchestration
that Broadway had always been known for.
The framework of the story was about three
couples in a small farm town in the Midwest
who separately move to New York and coincidentally meet. The plot moved through time

with them and was filled with revelations and great songs.

The evening was magical. Hopefully the pasta party the day after tomorrow would go as well.

Annie reached over and took Ash's hand. What she held was more than skin and bones. It was the magic of all life had to offer. Enough sunshine to shoo away the clouds. A whole new way of viewing life, of planning for the future, of accepting a gift that was being dangled in front of her. If only she'd grab it.

She replayed the night before last, when she'd been sitting naked on the side of his bed with the lights dimmed to shadows. How he'd come and stood in front of her. How she'd reached her hands up and painstakingly felt the pelvic bones that jutted out from his slim hips, wanting to feel every inch, how the smooth skin had rock hardness underneath. The hills and valleys of his flat belly. Her hands had reveled in the feeling, and then at holding his hips so she could keep him right there.

She had kissed those plains and rises, the way the bones and muscles folded toward her.

The tightness of his loins had all but twitched right in front of her. She'd bent her neck back to look up at him, his eyes hooded and slanted downward at her.

She'd wanted him to watch every one of her micromovements, how she'd stuck out her tongue as far as she could so that the very tip of it could flick the very tip of his sex. His moan had encouraged her to keep going so she'd repeated her motion. A hundred times. Then she'd let her tongue travel further along him and savored the buzz of his throb on her lips.

They had danced like that, with her taking more of him into her mouth and then sliding back only to do it again, and again, creating a beautiful rhythm. They'd ended up on the bed, wrapped in each other's arms and legs, forming themselves into all sorts of shapes and configurations, becoming wherever the next turn took them, Annie reaching a freedom she never knew was possible.

"We'll be making pasta today as we continue to celebrate Edward's retirement," Annie announced as she kicked off the pasta party class at Casa Greco, renowned chef Mino Greco's restaurant in Little Italy. The so-named downtown neighborhood had been settled by Italian immigrants. From the old days, Italian restaurants still drew tourists, especially with celebrity Greco on the map.

The kitchen had been fully prepped and readied for the pasta-making class. Although it was restaurant-size, it was no small feat making workstations for the thirty guests.

"*Congratulazioni*, Edward," Annie concluded.

Ash was off to the side but smiled at her offering of congratulations in Italian.

Edward was surrounded by his closest friends and some relatives who'd flown in for the week. Zara was out of town and missing the class, one less thing for Ash to be concerned about, though she'd be back on Saturday for the gala.

In front of each guest was an apron with an insignia stitched in to commemorate the occasion and the date. Everyone had a wooden cooking board and other kitchen implements, which each guest would take home as souvenirs, gifts that Annie had thought to provide. A few members of the restaurant staff were on hand, and they poured glasses of prosecco. "To Edward." Ash raised his class.

Murmurs of "to Edward" followed.

Ash took over. "We are so delighted to have this opportunity to cook with acclaimed chef Mino Greco." He pointed to the back entrance of the kitchen where Greco was supposed to enter from. All heads turned in that direction. Yet, there was no chef. Ash repeated with the gusto of an announcer, "Mino Greco!"

A pin drop could be heard in the kitchen. Ash's heart sank. It would be an utter disaster if the star chef didn't show up for this class. He knew Annie had verified every detail about the booking so this made no sense.

"Mino Greco!" he called out, as maybe the chef was behind the swinging kitchen doors waiting to be announced once again. "Chef Mino?"

"Alright, alright, stop yelling," Mino finally blasted through the doors. A big bearded man in a chef's coat, he barreled past the guests to the staging area in front.

Ash saw Annie's cheeks fill with air then deflate with relief. She put her hand over her heart.

Ash said, "Welcome, chef."

"Alright, you see all of these gadgets in front of you." Without any apology for being late or introduction to the party, class was underway. "Move them aside, today we will use only a rolling pin and the best tools, our two hands."

And the pasta making commenced. Ash lifted his prosecco glass with, "Cheers."

A half hour or so later, things were not going well.

"No, no, thin that dough out, it cannot cook like that," Mino berated Willy, a young man from Edward's most recent mentee group, now in their IT department. Apparently, he hadn't rolled out his pasta to the chef's specification. Willy used the heel of his hand to try to flatten the dough further.

Edward's inner circle of friends were chatting more than they were making pasta, as Chef Mino's disposition was a turnoff to many in the group. The chef didn't seem to care. When Ash walked by him to check on a couple of people, Mino hissed to him, "I get paid the same amount whether your guests are paying attention or not."

"He's awful," Annie whispered into Ash's ear when he stopped by her side.

"I know. And this whole thing was my idea. I can't even blame it on your predecessor, Marissa."

"It's me this is a bad reflection on. I wish I'd vetted him more carefully so I could have advised you."

"We figured all he had to do was make it a fun class. Nobody would really care if they learned anything or not."

"Stop, that's a ridiculous amount of lemon!" Mino seemed to be focusing his wrath on poor Willy, perhaps because he was one of the few still attentive to the lesson. The kid's eyes were saucers, the chef was stressing him out.

"You said we should add lemon zest to the ricotta ravioli filling to taste," Willy stated, half looking down for fear of another outburst.

"To taste! Not sores burned into the mouth from too much acid!" He pointed to the woman next to Willy, one of Edward's relatives. "And you, the opposite. Be aggressive with that pepper! We are not making food for babies!"

Ash's hackles rose. He knew men like the chef, men with thunderous voices, men who took the air out of the room and tried to make everyone else feel small. He had been raised by one of those men. In fact, he immediately wondered what Chef Mino's damage was, what made him how he was.

Chef Mino was not what met the eye. Not a big, kind nurturer. He was not a person to be allowed near someone else's emotions. Was anyone? Ash looked down to the floor and was overcome by the lost boy who couldn't depend on either his mother or the man he thought was his father.

Studying all of those couples at the Broadway evening, his core still hadn't understood how people could commit to staying together. How they relied on each other blindly, without fear. He doubted he was ever going to be one of those chosen for that. It was too late for him to change that much.

"Ash." Annie's soft voice made him lift his head from the pit it had fallen into. "What's wrong?"

"This." It wasn't the time to delve into Ash's demons. It was easier to blame his distress on the failed class. He waved his arm across the kitchen. Edward and a few people were talking work, 401(k)s and annuities. Everyone else looked either bored or deflated.

Annie said, "I have an idea." She began

furiously punching into her phone. Within fifteen minutes, she was leading the thirty guests out of the kitchen and through the front door of Casa Greco, as the famous chef merely watched the parade and yelled at individual people, "Go, that's fine. Go."

As if lured by a pied piper, the group followed Annie half a block to Il Padrone, where the manager she'd just spoken on the phone with was waiting at the door with open arms. "*Benvenuto* everyone, come in, come in. We are putting tables together so you can eat family style."

"Thank you for helping us out on such short notice," Annie said to the manager as everyone filed in.

Many bottles of Chianti later, bellies filled with meats and red sauce, the guests' laughter filled the dining room. Annie had salvaged what could have been a disaster. For Edward's guests, the fiasco with Chef Greco was already irrelevant.

Except to Ash, who would apparently receive reminders everywhere he turned that people wounded each other and he should never get close to them.

CHAPTER TEN

"CAN YOU ZIP me into this?" Annie approached Ash in his dressing area.

"My pleasure." He figured she'd traveled from her guest space across the living room to his master suite all the while holding up her gown to keep it from falling off her. She was barefoot and had curlers in her hair. She turned her back to him, to show him the long zipper. A thin bra under the dress crossed her shoulder blades. The bra was a strapless style made of what looked to be the same silky fabric as the wisp of underwear she wore, a tan color no doubt chosen so it wouldn't show from under her gown. "How do I do it?"

She laughed and he saw her sweet smile in the reflection of the mirror facing him. "You have to pick up both sides of the gown and then start zipping from the bottom."

"And I do that with my third hand?"

She laughed again and the sound of it was like music.

He knew what she meant in theory. He brought the two sides of the garment to each other so that he could begin at the bottom of the zipper, which met where her lower back curved like a flower stem. He'd kissed her naked back and would love to do it again but, obviously, this wasn't the right time and he had a task ahead of him, working inch by inch to envelope her in this golden gown they'd bought a few weeks ago at Bergen's when they'd decided her *image* needed a makeover.

He'd had some resistance, finding her natural beauty more alluring than this artful construction, but he understood the need for the change and it was successful. People treated her with reverence as the esteemed colleague from Denver who was brought in to clean up the faulty work of a fired outsource. Those at the pasta party really got to see her in action when she salvaged the botched class and quickly arranged a dinner where the wine was flowing and everything was funny.

She wore all of these fine new clothes— they didn't wear her. It wasn't a little girl's dress-up game. The way she'd taken charge of this retirement week for Edward had been a sight to behold, and one to be proud of. Just as he'd imagined, several of his VPs and board members noticed.

Their eyes locked in the mirror as his hands continued to inch up the gown's zipper. He'd been pushing away the reality that, if they stuck to the original plan, next week they'd begin a new charade, no longer posing as a couple so in love many onlookers must have thought they were on the verge of a lifelong commitment. Next week it would be time for the final act in the masquerade. The cordial breakup that Annie had decided upon. Ash had done his best to avoid thinking about the post-gala realities. And, in fact, he was going to continue to push it all away tonight. Except it was on his mind. Because he was torn in every direction wanting to let the game continue while also advising himself to cut her loose before they could find a way to hurt each other, which he still thought was inevitable.

"You're not catching any of the fabric into the zipper are you?" She motioned like she was trying to look behind her to see what he was doing. "Go slowly. It's very delicate."

His mouth tipped up. "Indeed."

Once the zipper project had been completed, Annie turned around. "Mission accomplished."

"That dress looks spectacular on you."

"Thank you."

He was suddenly tongue-tied, not wanting to talk about anything real so they both stood awkwardly in the center of his dressing area. One wall was a full-length closet, dozens of suits arranged in order of hue from the tuxedos on the left followed by the blackest fabrics all the way through browns, blues and grays to the far end with rarely worn beiges and whites. The perpendicular wall was lined with shelves. Rows of dress shirts were stacked neatly in order of solids and patterns, each with a gossamer ribbon tied on by the launderers. There were casual shirts on hangers, and then more stacks of T-shirts, polo shirts and pullovers. Tie racks. The bottom half of that closet held the shoe racks. Dress shoes, casual shoes, boots, sports shoes, sneakers, footwear for extreme weather. Another closet held athletic wear. There were coats and jackets, rain gear. Drawers filled with pajamas, underwear and socks. Glass cases with watches, cufflinks, rows of sunglasses.

He'd certainly done well for himself. And yet none of the *stuff* meant anything. Life wasn't about T-shirts and cedar closets. Maybe he didn't even know the real meaning of life, but he knew for him it wasn't material items.

Agitated, he tightened his bow tie and then reached for his tuxedo jacket. "We should get going."

"What's wrong?"

"Nothing."

The black SUV was waiting for them in the building's garage. "Sir." The driver nodded then adjusted his cap. "Ma'am." He opened the passenger door wide so that Annie could maneuver her dress into the seat. Ash entered from the other side so that Annie didn't have to push in any further than necessary. He knew the drill, charity affairs and women in gowns. This was his first time with a pretend girlfriend, though.

As the driver pulled into formidable evening traffic, Annie's beauty quelled his restlessness. He couldn't take his eyes off her, the colored lights of the city at night illuminating her with one hue or the next. Her shiny hair was done in a style that lifted some of it on each side and the rest down in golden strands. She was resplendent. Still not any more so than when she was scrubbed clean and naked but, nonetheless, he knew she'd be the most beautiful woman in the ballroom tonight.

"Do you want a drink?" He gestured to the pull-out tray between the two of them that held a bottle of champagne.

"No, I want to stay sharp. There are a lot of moving pieces tonight."

Had they picked the day that Annie was going to announce she and Ash had broken up? No. The plan had never been that thorough, a fact he was now berating himself for. He hadn't thought the charade through to the end. At first, he'd acted on impulse, so tired of fighting off Zara. Then the scheme to pretend he and Annie were together had taken on a life of its own. They'd been granted Edward's, and everyone else's, blessing.

Now they moved as a couple, they thought as a couple. Then the kisses in public became private, as well. It all felt right, it all felt organic. What kind of mess had he created? In a million years he wouldn't have imagined that real feelings would grow. Their past wasn't supposed to have relevance to their present.

To make things even more complicated, he'd promised her the new job. She'd certainly proved this week how much EJ needed someone at the helm of event productions; her promotion would be a good move for the company. With their relationship lined up on so many levels they'd have to find a way to break it all apart and keep only the right aspects.

Maybe it would be a good idea to headquarter the position in Dubai after all, their second-largest office after New York. Many thousands of miles away. At least for the first year so that they could separate the jumble they'd gotten themselves into. If she was amenable to that. A tug in his chest didn't like anything about that plan. *One thing at a time*, he admonished himself. *Get through tonight.*

"Edward has now helped three generations of our family achieve our financial goals," a client announced while shaking Ash's hand as soon as he and Annie arrived. She quickly dashed off to make sure everything was in order in the kitchen.

"I'm glad to hear that, Mr. Nevel. And I

hope we'll continue together for generations more."

"May you have children who grow up to take your place when the time comes."

Children. Ash had never, ever imagined having children. Wasn't it the common wisdom that hurt people hurt people? He'd be no good to anyone, least of all a child who'd have innocent trust in him for guidance and protection. A child of his wouldn't even know who they were, just as Ash would never know who his true father was. And all he had as an example was a mean and vindictive man who'd taught Ash absolutely nothing about life, about love, about anything. No, Ash was his own sad legacy, it began and ended with him.

Although, something else had developed. The scheme to pretend to be together had changed him. Annie had shown him how sharing a moment, a sunset, a vision, a spontaneous kiss added up to a life. That without someone else, walking the path alone hurt even more.

He needed more. He needed Annie.

He caught sight of her talking to a group of wait staff. She was utterly breathtaking, her sparkling eyes shining even from a distance.

If only they'd both been raised in different environments. In a parallel universe where they could both trust love, they could have built a life together. But she'd been damaged as much as he had. A father who cheated, who didn't appreciate the woman he married or the children that union bore, had left her with wounds still as tender as Ash's were.

Even if he was able to leave his past in the wind, and take that giant gamble that he could put his pain behind him, was she? She'd stayed in Denver where all of her memories still breathed. She'd said her mother and her brothers didn't have healthy relationships, either. Had she evolved enough to take her own shot, to try to prove the odds wrong? Had what they'd shared these past weeks together washed them clean?

And if she was able, she could do better than him. She shouldn't depend on him. Because he could say unequivocally that he was not past his hurt, he was not over and on top of the daily demons that wrestled to bring him down. He'd learned to push them aside when needed and to be a success in business. That wasn't the same as committing to an intimate union, one that might have the potential to last forever. His ghosts still controlled him.

Plus, he could still turn out to be a monster like Karl was, his psyche learning from the past. Odds weren't good on him, she could find a more reliable deal elsewhere. He wanted her to have a shot at happiness and peace. He wanted that for her so much that he'd sacrifice it himself, to make sure of not hurting her.

Easily, he'd give up whatever hope he had that he could be with her for real. He'd trade it in a minute to increase her chances. He didn't want to hold her back.

"You finally pulled yourself out of the kitchen," Ash greeted Annie when she found him in the thick of the gala, chitchatting with three beautiful women in designer gowns. He bowed his head to his guests and said, "Excuse me."

"We are rolling." She was glad he'd immediately pulled away from those women although a little surge of emotion jacked through her that he was in such company in the first place.

"I see the waitstaff is passing hors d'oeuvres. Old-school, like you wanted."

"I thought it would be fun to do a throwback dinner. That's why the filet mignon with whipped potatoes."

"And hors d'oeuvres of little crispy fried things that no one knows what they actually are but they taste delicious."

She smiled. "Although look at my wine fountains." She pointed at the circles of well-dressed guests surrounding the color-ful wines. They were a success.

"Let's go say hi to the Shellmans. They're a big account." He took her hand for the first time since they'd arrived. She'd been behind the scenes, solving a problem with the band's stage setup, having a pep talk with the staff, giving the chef final approvals. There hadn't been any time yet for her to put on her Ash's girlfriend hat.

As he guided her toward the Shellmans, Annie did feel like a fairy-tale princess at the ball. Well, a princess in charge of the ball. Nonetheless, she was in this gorgeous gown with this spectacular man in this daz-zling city. The man that had always been her most cherished fantasy, and her most closely guarded secret. His sure hand holding hers sent a swirl down her spine. She knew she'd react to his touch for as long as she lived.

"Ron and Hilary Shellman, this is my girl-friend, Annie Butterfield."

"Nice to meet you."

"Ash!" A stately woman with heavy red lip-stick approached, lopsidedly holding a glass of the merlot. "I wanted to ask your advice about my account."

No sooner had Ash fielded her than two other women, one older and one younger approach. "Ash," said the older, "you remember my daughter Gigi, don't you?"

She heard a voice from behind her, "Now, Ash Moretti. That's husband material."

As Annie watched the spectacle, Ash's disdain at the attention of woman after woman was palpable. If she sensed him correctly, he hated having them throw themselves at him,. Or, worse still, pushy grandfathers and aunties offering up their eligible young females. The last thing he considered himself was *husband material*. In fact, it was because of Zara's unrelenting advances that Ash created the charade with Annie in the first place.

The truth rained down on her like a storm. There was nowhere to run for cover. If during this time with Ash she'd genuinely had a moment's thought that her playacting could become permanent, she needed to have her head examined. Ash wasn't made for a forever with one person. All of these hopeful women didn't know half of what Annie did, the long list of reasons why they were wasting their time.

The original plan was for the happy couple to break up, at her instigation, after this gala. Somehow, though, they were to remain friendly so that he could offer her that VP position that would keep her in New York. Supposing that was easier than it sounded, how long would it be before Ash asked one of the beautiful women he encountered to share an evening, or perhaps a hotel night, with him? That was what he did; that was how he filled in the gap for human contact that despite his unhappy childhood, he still needed a taste of. Fair enough. She'd have no claim to him once the fake couple broke up.

Was she supposed to move to New York and watch all of that in action day after day, year after year? She wasn't strong enough for that, to see every day the one thing she'd always wanted withheld from her, punishing her for wanting it. As much as she was poised to ascend in her professional life, there were limits to her courage. No, the solution was Dubai, which was a better place to hide than Denver. That would be the compromise.

The band started up, Ash's eyes darted over to them as they started in on a popular ballad that spoke of romantic devotion.

"Let's dance," he said to Annie, nodding to the Shellmans. "Have a lovely evening."

She didn't know what had been going on in his mind the past few days, although she sensed it must be matters as serious as what was going through hers. They'd worked like mad to pull off this week of events and here they were, with the culmination of the gala. With their future uncertain. Yet as he took her by the hand and led her onto the dance floor, she willed all the problems to slip away. For a fleeting moment. She just wanted to be in the now, in the *what if*, in the *if only*. To be a woman in a beautiful gown dancing securely with her man.

He brought her right into the center of the dance floor, with other couples all around them, just where they'd kissed on that first night. He swooped his other hand around her waist and brought her close to him. Her head fit so perfectly in the crook of his neck. He smelled so good, fresh and clean and familiar.

Their bodies connected together becoming one unit. They locked into place and while Annie had never learned ballroom dancing, it came easily to feel Ash's legs against hers and to instinctively know how to follow his moves, like his DNA code had already imprinted on her. Which, after all this time, it had.

When his foot moved forward hers moved back. When she felt the slight pressure of his arm or his hipbone for her to follow, she did. As they swayed and glided and claimed the little area of the dance floor as theirs, Annie all but swooned.

She could believe in this exact moment that she had arrived. She was no longer incomplete. In Ash's arms she couldn't fail; her orbit was limitless. She kept telling herself to indulge in the fantasy, to hang on, because it might be the last time she ever would.

They continued through another song. Her feet barely touched the ground. During one moment, she pulled back and away, as if she just needed to check the surroundings. And also, as lovely as it was to bring her face into his neck and against his chest, she wanted to see his face.

She'd hoped to look into his eyes and know that he was feeling the same closeness, the same destiny that she was, the certainty she'd been carrying around for ten years. Yet when she looked up at him, his eyes darted in one direction and then another—he refused to make contact with hers. "Ash?"

He didn't have to answer. She understood the pallor across his face. Her heart fell to the floor into a million pieces that pooled at her feet. Because she'd been trying to avoid what she knew in her soul was true. This was as far as Ash would ever go. The make-believe domesticity. The dark nights confiding in each other. The seamless way they'd come to guess each other's thoughts. The moonlit midnights of making love like their lives depended on it.

None of that was sustainable. Even though if she thought that she might be able to walk beside him while the past got smaller and more distant until it maybe even disappeared, he couldn't.

How would she survive this? She knew she had to lay it all on the table. He had to have all of the facts. She had to tell him her truth—it was the only way she would be able to continue on. And it had to be right now, before shame and disappointment would render her silent. "Ash." She had to speak fairly loud over the music. "I know that the time has come for us to stop pretending to be together. We did what we intended to do. And to continue is not fair to you, it's not fair to Edward, and it's not fair to me."

"Yes, we'll make the announcement next week," he said sadly, gravely, his face fallen.

"I want to tell you something. I'm in love with you. And I didn't just fall in love with you since I've been back in New York. I've been in love with you since I first got to know you ten years ago. All of this time. I need you to hold that and for both of us to accept it as a truth that can't be ignored, in order for me to move past it. I don't know how we carry on from here. I do know I can't pretend to have stopped loving you after only pretending to have started loving you in the first place, while secretly loving you for real all along."

"Oh, Annie."

As a single tear dripped down her face, she knew she couldn't stay on the dance floor with its prying eyes any longer. She had to collect herself and finish the evening. She told herself she could fall apart afterward. Right now, she had to get away from him for a minute. "Excuse me." She removed herself from Ash's grasp, which was as painful as ripping off a full-body bandage. She turned away and headed for the grand staircase that led to the hotel lobby. Holding on to the wooden carved banister she ascended the stairs, sensing that Ash was watching, the train of her golden gown floating behind her, until she was out of sight.

CHAPTER ELEVEN

BEFORE ASH COULD even begin to react, Edward was at his shoulder.

"I'm so glad you found *the one*," he said to Ash over the din of the gala in action.

The two men stood side by side watching Annie, followed by the train of her gown, glide up the marble staircase. Although Edward's words did not fit with the moment at hand, Ash answered in a faraway voice, just wanting to appease him. "Yes, the one." He'd tell Edward at the right time that they were just acting in a charade.

Despite his mentor's presence beside him, Ash was in a trance as he watched Annie not just go up the staircase and disappear from view but, he suspected, from his life. The change had happened. He'd pictured a carefully scripted and orchestrated announcement that they had broken up, with a plan to go for-

ward as colleagues. Not an emotionally devastating real-life ripping apart that he knew
he'd never recover from.

"Hi A-ash," Zara cooed, suddenly by Edward's other side, no doubt noticing the men
together and seizing on the moment. "Where's
Annie going?" she asked mischievously.

Truth was, Ash didn't know where Annie
was going. The consummate professional, she
wasn't leaving the hotel or doing anything
that would shirk her many duties for the rest
of the evening. He could only surmise that she
needed a moment to herself. However, he did
have to quickly figure out what needed to be
done if she actually did leave.

He knew he couldn't stand any longer to
be in the center of the dance floor where that
first night they kissed, the kiss that turned the
world on its axis. The kiss that had led to a
thousand more. That he'd grown accustomed
to, that now he couldn't imagine his life without even though he knew he'd have to.

"I've got to check on something, pardon
me," he said to Edward, nodding his head to
Zara.

Ash maneuvered his way through the crowd,
helloing as need be. He found the party man-

ager and checked in with her, then rushed into the kitchen to see the head chef. He swerved back into the ballroom and then bounded up the staircase, hoping none of the guests gave any thought to one then the other of them exiting the party. He needed to try to find Annie, if she was still on the premises.

She said she'd been in love with him for ten years.

Careening across the hotel lobby and down a corridor of locked rooms, he swiped the key card on the fleet of offices they'd rented for the party. Flipping on the lights he found them empty. Across the hall were a couple of guest rooms they'd taken as well in case Edward or other members of his family or inner circle needed a private space. Those, too, were vacant.

She'd loved him since the beginning.

He dashed his way back to the lobby and out the hotel's front doors, where uniformed bell captains held the doors open and assisted guests in and out of cars and taxis. Not caring that he was the only one on the scene in a tuxedo, he surveyed the entire porte cochere area. He took note of the voices of many people and the crisp fresh air of the New York evening. He and Annie had been indoors for hours.

He wouldn't have blamed her if she'd come out for a breather. Not wanting to reveal who he or Annie were he asked a bellman, "Have you seen a woman in a gold ball gown about five feet tall with blond hair?"

"I haven't, sir." Annie would have been noticeable, dressed as she was. And this was the only way in or out of the hotel, so she was most likely still inside. As he walked back in, another idea hit him.

He wasn't wrong. He spotted her on the terrace of the Garden Room, where they'd had dinner the first night after she'd arrived from Denver. The greenhouse beyond the glass walls was lit with its usual fairy lights and pools of flowers creating a blast of colors. He swept alongside the dining room to reach the access door and stepped out into the space that Annie rightly found so magical on their previous visit here. It was, in fact, a magical garden of almost celestial pleasure, especially when he caught sight of Annie, standing under an arbor and gazing outward. Her dress swayed with the light breeze and wisps of her hair glistened in the light.

She'd held her love in secret.

"Annie," he called out. Her head turned ever so slightly indicating that she'd heard him, but she chose not to turn around.

He came closer as she must have known he would. When he reached the arbor he stepped beside her. They stood side by side looking out at the rest of the greenhouse and beyond to the city lights. "Have you left the gala?" She was still desperately needed, there was dessert and the auction to supervise and he didn't imagine she'd abandon her post, although he couldn't be sure.

"Certainly not. I just needed a minute. I'll come back in."

"Is there something more you want to say to me?"

She loved him.

She'd already told him that she'd been in love with him for ten years. It wasn't like he expected her to have more, but if she did, he wanted to hear it.

"I think I've said it all." His heart told him that what she wanted was for him to say something back to her. That his feelings matched hers. That he was madly in lo… He couldn't even allow it in his head, let alone say it out loud. He wasn't entitled to that kind of emotion, never had been, never would be. Regardless of the pit in his stomach screaming at him to be honest about what he desired. Needed, in fact.

"I'm sorry, Annie." He had to respond. He owed her that. "In all honesty I've never felt like I even wanted to be with someone like that, except with you. I don't know if you feel able now to commit your heart and put your past in a box. I wish *I* could, but I know I can't. If you can, I wish you all the happiness in the world. You deserve it."

She used a finger to swipe under one eye and then the other. She was crying. "I know, Ash. We're just doing the best we can."

He felt like crying too, but he wasn't free enough to shed tears. "I wish I could do better for you. I'm sure if I was with someone, I'd be waiting for the other shoe to drop. I'm ruined for trust."

She snickered. "We're quite a pair."

"We always were."

Was he really letting this happen, letting the most complete connection he'd ever had in his life slip away? Was he, in the end, such a coward that he was going to cut himself off before he got even deeper and even more invested? Why wouldn't he just jump in? It couldn't possibly hurt more than losing her.

"What happens now?"

He was sure she must feel as he did that it was going to be difficult if not impossible to erase these past few weeks and create a new relationship at EJ. "Do you want to go back to Denver for a little while and we'll define the VP position before we need you to start?" His lungs ached at *before we need you*. In reality, he needed her every day. After life as a *we* it was going to be a bitter nothingness to go back to being a *me*.

She dipped her head once in a nod of agreement.

"We'll stick to the original plan." She smoothed down the bodice of her gown. She swept a hand across the back of her neck, no doubt to tame any errant hairs. She was preparing to go back into battle, to the gala.

Ash bit his lip, his insides turning to stone.

Annie embarked on one of the hardest things she'd ever had to do. It was one thing putting on a happy face when she didn't feel well or was tired. But to face five hundred people at the gala when her heart had just shattered like a thousand shards of broken glass was unimaginable. Although she'd do it. Partially because she couldn't let this crush her to death. She also had to pull herself together because she wanted to do it for Edward, who'd given so much to so many. And yes, she wanted to do it for Ash, to whom Edward had given possibly the greatest gift a person could bestow on someone. Edward loved Ash, and for that Annie would be eternally grateful.

"Shall we go back?" Ash held his hand out.

"Yes. Is dessert being served?" She took the firm hand that had touched every inch of her body. It was a hand she would forever wish to have in hers, but it was clearer now than it had ever been that that was never to be.

"They were just starting." Ash led her quickly out of the greenhouse, through the restaurant and down the elevator to the main floor of the ballroom, bypassing the stairs she'd just fled up in a state of overwhelm.

As they walked into the ballroom, several heads turned. Older people, no doubt clients, gave pleased smiles, appreciating seeing Annie and Ash as a young couple in love.

Annie surveyed the room. For whatever

reason, the waitstaff were uneven in service. Some tables already had plates of dessert in front of each guest. At those tables waiters were already pouring coffee. While tables on the other side of the room hadn't received their trio of tarts, one mandarin orange with dark chocolate, one crème brûlée with berries and one salted caramel hazelnut.

She let go of Ash's hand, a separation they both looked down to notice, and then dashed into the dessert kitchen to see if there was a bigger problem underlying the error in timing. It had been a nearly flawless evening that she didn't want to see go downhill now. It was bad enough that she'd had to remove herself from the ballroom to take a personal moment.

"I apologize." The head waiter was sincere when questioned. "We simply got a late start brewing the coffee. There were a lot of special requests on the entrées."

"Ladies and gentlemen, we'll begin our live auction in a few minutes," the auctioneer announced through a handheld microphone. "Please find your numbered paddle on the table beside you, and verify that it has your name." The room buzzed as people shifted their chairs to face the stage. Coffee service continued until every guest had been offered a cup.

After making her rounds, Annie spotted Ash in the crowd, leaning over at a table to talk to three men. He looked so focused and powerful, the men engaged in talking to him. She hadn't been wrong to pine over him for all these years. He was worth it.

"Ladies and gentlemen, we begin with item number fifteen in the catalogue, the Cape Cod house. This thirty-two-thousand-square-foot beach house has five bedrooms, three with balconies overlooking the water and the other two open to rolling hills. Wonderful for a family reunion, a gathering of friends or a personal retreat. Our donor is generously allowing you to reserve a one-week stay. Bidding begins at one hundred thousand."

Annie saw guests from all over the ballroom raise their paddles at the opening bid. The auctioneer continued. "Do I have two hundred thousand?" A few paddles went up, not as many as the first time. "Two hundred thousand. Can we go two hundred fifty thousand?" Fewer still but active.

Annie looked over at Ash who had backed up against one of the pillars with his arms folded across his chest. She wanted more than anything to walk over there and stand next to him so they could watch together as loads of money was raised for the teen summer program Edward cared so deeply about. But she couldn't. By Ash's side may have been where she thought she belonged. She'd gotten a taste of what that was like, a well she wanted to drink from for all of her life. But that wasn't to be.

"Can I get three hundred thousand?" The auctioneer persisted. "Three? Two fifty going to number sixty-seven. Two fifty. Going once. Going twice. Sold."

Annie would get on a plane in the morning. Just as Ash had suggested, nothing needed to be announced or even decided upon right away. She'd lick her wounds in her home town, away from prying eyes. She wanted the powers that be at EJ to create that job for her one way or another. And in order to get it, she was going to have to release the hold Ash had on her. He could never give her what she wanted and wished for from him. It was her problem, not his.

"Welcome to Denver International Airport." The pilot's voice confirmed the landing of the plane. Annie had spent the flight reviewing the speakers' schedule and staffing for an upcoming educational seminar in Seattle. The past weeks had been so focused on the events for Edward's retirement, she needed to work double time to catch up on all of her other projects.

Working during the flight also helped her keep her mind off Ash. Although that was a lie because it was more like the other way around, that work occasionally distracted her from the agony of separation that tore at her. Something she hoped would lessen in time. Even if the torch she'd held for Ash was as bright and sturdy as Lady Liberty's had been in New York.

"Hi, Mom, I'm home." As soon as the driver dropped her off at her house, she phoned to let her mom know she was back. "I'll come by tomorrow."

She'd never shared anything about her feelings for Ash with her family. With the tone her father had set for the Butterfield household, people kept to themselves. That was their mode of operation. Full stop. She supposed she could reach out to a friend and unpack the many things that had happened in the past few weeks. But it really wasn't in her nature to share her internal life with anyone. Besides Ash, of course, with whom she wanted to discuss everything.

She changed into a comfortable lounge outfit, no longer caring how she was dressed. In a cupboard she found some microwaveable popcorn and opened a bottle of wine. Wasn't that what unattached professional women had for dinner, popcorn and wine? She snickered at labeling herself a cliché. She liked her house and had worked hard to make enough money to buy it. Usually after she came home from a trip, she surveyed everything. The Victorian architecture, the big bay windows, the moldings, the fireplace. Somehow tonight it just seemed empty. A collection of items that no longer mattered to her.

She flipped on the television and watched the local news. Tiring of that, she shut off all the lights and got into bed. When she closed her eyes, it didn't sound like New York from the thirty-ninth floor, a particular din she'd gotten quite used to.

Her phone dinged, which made her eyes pop open. She leaned over to reach for it. A message from Ash. Just want to know you got to Denver okay. She sent an affirming emoji and then clicked the screen off.

She drove herself to the office in the morning, realizing that she hadn't driven a car in weeks. Annoying morning traffic gave her the thought that she wouldn't mind not having to drive everywhere. Cities like New York certainly had that advantage.

"Hey, Annie, how was New York?" She received her first greeting at the office.

"Hi, Annie."

"That breakfast event with all the EJ staff around the world was fun."

It was nice that the Denver employees welcomed her back. She slipped into her office, with its pretty vista out the window of the ground floor landscaping. She'd scheduled a couple of in-person meetings today and would spend the morning getting updates.

Yes, work. It would be her solace. It always had been. Months and years from now, what had happened in the past few weeks would be a distant memory.

She didn't believe that for a second, but perhaps if she said it to herself enough times she would.

Checking her texts, she saw one from Ash. She tapped it open to read, How is it being back?

She wanted to respond, IF YOU'RE NOT GOING TO LOVE ME, LET ME BE! But she needed to relearn how to deal with him while keeping her emotions out of it so she tapped back with another emoji.

Without waiting to discuss it with anyone, Ash included, she sent an email to Edward. She and Ash had decided to remain esteemed colleagues and dear friends but were going their separate ways personally and were no longer a couple. She just wanted to be done with it. Edward sent a reply saying he was sorry to hear it, and had thought they were wonderful together. His disappointment seared. But there was nothing to do but move forward. With any luck she'd be in a VP position soon where she and Ash would find a way to genuinely be the amicable exes and coworkers they claimed they would.

The day flew by and she stopped at a Mexican restaurant known for their take-out food. She ordered an assortment for her, her mother and her brothers whom she was meeting for dinner.

As soon as she drove into the driveway of

her childhood home, a feeling of dread came over her. It was as if she was back there, with that terrible apprehension of not knowing what she was to find inside. Would her mother be sitting at the kitchen table trying to muffle her cries because she'd just heard of her husband's latest betrayal?

Often her mother would find out from a neighbor or a mom at school who'd tell her that they'd spotted her husband at a bar across town or a motel parking lot twenty miles down on the interstate. Or she'd find out because she'd looked at her husband's phone, maybe to read a telling text or simply an unusual phone number called over and over again. In any case, any day might be the one that betrayal and deceit was discovered while Annie and her brothers were at school.

Or would she come home to a day in between infidelities when they were just a family of five who had almost nothing to say to each other? When a series of grunts and shrugs constituted dinner conversation, after which everyone would retreat to their separate silos. The kids to the den for homework. Annie's dad, if he wasn't going out, would open a beer and sit in the living room, perhaps flipping through a magazine. And her mom, under the guise of doing the dinner dishes, would basically hide in the kitchen until bedtime. Annie remembered the *click* sound of the bottle of her mom's sleeping pills, one taken before bed every night.

"Hi, Mom." Annie entered, toting her bags of enchiladas, tacos and burritos.

"Hi."

"Hey, Joey. Hey, Stu," she greeted her brothers who were in the den watching TV. They didn't hug because, well, they didn't hug.

"How was the Big Apple?"

"It was…" Her first response was to say great, but it was more complicated than that. It had been awful, too. She and her one true love had not ridden off on a white horse together. Even her fake one true love was no longer on the horse. "… Interesting" was what she arrived at to answer the question.

"I'm hungry," Stu chimed in, not paying attention to her answer.

Her mom put paper plates and plastic utensils down on the dining table which had the same stained tablecloth on it that she remembered from the last time she was over.

"How's work?" Annie asked Joey, who had

just gotten a new job at a home improvement store. He'd had some previous trouble with substance abuse and hadn't been able to keep a job long.

"My boss is a jerk." Oh, so he'd soon be adding this one to his former employers list.

"Stu, what's new with you?" Annie was trying.

"Nothing. Same ol' same ol'." It was hard to believe she'd grown up in a house full of people who knew so little about who each other truly was, or cared.

After dinner she wandered into her old bedroom. It had become a hodgepodge. Her Mom used part of it to hold laundry baskets. The nightstands on both sides of the bed were cluttered with a half dozen lamps each, all old and unwanted. Annie's bed hadn't changed, the same rose print comforter she'd gotten when she moved into her college dorm that she brought back after graduation, before the year she spent in EJ's program where housing and linen were provided.

A small basket on the dresser held several of her old headbands. She used to wear those every day. To keep the hair out of her eyes, but somehow to hold her back, too. They were a sort of disguise.

The room felt stifling, claustrophobic. She couldn't think of a happy memory here; the best she could do were ones that were *not terrible*, remembering summertime when the kids in the neighborhood would ride bikes, cool off with garden hoses and be allowed to stay out until the streetlights came on at sundown. Not much, but it was something.

She deserved better in every facet of her life. This rose-print comforter in her mother's house shouldn't be Annie's destiny. She knew what she needed to do. It was time to claim what was hers.

The housekeeper let Ash into Edward's Upper East Side home. After crossing the entrance hall filled with a combination of fine art and personal photos on the walls, he stepped into the living room. The gleaming baby grand piano where virtuoso Edward sat many an hour was the focal point. The polished floors and clusters of furniture were tasteful.

Edward ambled down the stairs, relaxed in a pair of jeans, shirt not tucked in. He hugged his successor with the warmth that he'd always bestowed on Ash. "If I didn't thank you enough already for that beautiful send-off, let me say it again."

"You're welcome, but I think you have Annie to thank as much as me." Which brought them to the reason Ash decided to visit Edward in person rather than talk over the phone or on a video call.

They sat at a couple of high-backed armchairs with a table in between.

"Do you want something to eat or drink?"

"No, but thanks."

"Your voice sounds somber. I was sorry to hear from Annie that the two of you were announcing a split."

"That's what I need to talk to you about."

"Alright."

"Annie and I were never really together. That is to say, it didn't start out that way."

"Go on." Edward leaned forward, elbows on the arms of his chair.

"I was hoping not to have to tell you this, but my deception feels wrong. It started with Zara."

"Zara?" Edward was clearly rightly bewildered, wondering what his stepdaughter would have to do with anything.

"Zara had developed a little crush on me and was constantly coming around the office unannounced."

"She was?" Edward's eyebrows scrunched.

"I didn't want to embarrass you about it so I thought I could fix it on my own. When I brought Annie to New York to help with your retirement week, I thought she could be a buffer and get Zara to back off. When that didn't work, I had an impulsive idea to pretend that Annie and I were together. Which worked, and Zara stopped coming around."

"You should have told me. I'd have spoken to her."

"I should have. But I wanted everything perfect for your retirement and for you to not have to worry about anything."

"I'll make sure Zara has no reason to be at the office ever again. Silly girl. I apologize that you had to go through that nonsense."

Next came the hard part. "The plan was that after the parties, Annie would announce, as she did, that we had broken up. And no one would be the wiser that we weren't together in the first place."

"Which would have been fine," Edward

said as he raised his finger in the air, "except that it wasn't fake between you and Annie."

"How did you know that?"

"Oh, please, Ash, it's clear as day that the two of you are in love. Your eyes light up when the other walks into a room. When you take a step, she takes one in response and vice versa. And the two of you at the gala on the dance floor, like something out of a fairy tale."

Ash hadn't considered that they were only too good at the roles they were playing. The more real they had seemed to onlookers, the better. "Hmm."

"So. What is this nonsense about breaking up? Why on earth would you let go of what you found, what I suspect began ten years ago?" Edward's wisdom was disturbing. Ash felt so bad for Edward's loss of his love. If you were devoted to someone, you had to risk the possibility of many kinds of loss. Edward's was the harshest, to prematurely lose his love to death. The world was fragile. Nothing could ever be taken for granted. "Have you only now realized that you love her?"

"I love her?" Ash knew those words to be true yet couldn't believe he'd said those words out loud. But as soon as he did he felt like a bird whose wings had been bound but were suddenly set free. "I love her." *I love her!*

"Of course you do."

Of course he did.

Now what?

Rather than calling for a driver, Ash left Edward's house on foot to walk the streets of the city.

On every block, there was joy and sorrow, triumph and disappointment. That was life. The pain he was experiencing at the real breakup of the not-fake couple couldn't be any worse than anything else that might happen if he opened his soul to Annie. He couldn't go on like this. Without her, any progress he'd made on his life's journey was destroyed. He couldn't walk the city streets or run a billion-dollar company with a hole this big in his heart.

There was only one choice.

Edward's words rang again in Ash's ears, reassuring him as he looked out the airplane window at powdery blue skies and puffs of clouds on the way to Denver. Edward, who even with his devastating outcome wouldn't have traded being in love for anything. Ash was in love, a fact already known by Edward and, apparently, half the free world. Ash Moretti was lucky to love Annie Butterfield and he wouldn't take that love for granted. He was ready to hire a skywriter, or to carve it into a tree trunk.

He didn't just love her. He was head over heels in love with her and intended to be by her side for the rest of their lives. Just like the couples he hadn't been able to take his eyes off at the parties and the gala. Couples that had been through good and bad, thick and thin, but had vowed to stay together no matter what.

"What are you doing here?" Annie was stunned after she opened the front door to her house, which was up a few outdoor stairs that he had bounded. "Why didn't you call?"

Her questions took him aback because, had he been of sound mind, he should have called, emailed, texted, *something* before bolting to the airport, hopping on a plane, flagging a taxi and using Annie's EJ employee file to find her home address. It was only that when he'd been with Edward and found himself able in an instant to accept what he had been denying his heart, he just wanted to get to Annie as soon as possible and start righting wrongs. He hadn't even considered what he would have done if she hadn't been home. "Can I come in?"

"Yes." He took that as a victory and starting point. She opened wide the big blue door with its smoked-glass panels and tacitly entered onto her hardwood floors, still only in the doorway. The first thing he saw inside was the wood banister, painted white, that led to a second floor.

"I'd never pictured what your house would be like. It's nice."

"Ash, why are you here without letting me know you were coming?"

"Because I love you. And I wasn't going to tell you that over the phone or in a text."

Annie froze, her hand still wrapped around the brass knob of her front door. She looked at him with glassy eyes, as if she was frightened. "After I told you that I'd been in love with you for all these years, it felt like you rejected me."

"I had a gut reaction. You said it as a matter of fact. With sureness. The first thing I thought of was what if you stopped? I couldn't take it."

"So you'll protect yourself. That makes sense. It's a smart move. You always make the right choices."

That was painful for Ash to hear. He'd hurt her with his defensiveness to her decade-old admission. And now she was the one protecting herself. She'd loved him from afar, from within a dream. She'd never had to trust him.

"I think you rejected me, too. That's not what I want."

Their eyes locked, both of them carrying under their skin all of what and who they were. He wanted to reach for her, to hold her tight, to take her pain away, which might take away his in the process. But he didn't get a smoke signal to move forward. Her eyes told him not to come closer. A cloud moved in the sky bringing a change to the lighting.

Finally, she broke the moment. "Oh, come inside for heaven's sake."

He entered all the way and she closed the door behind him. He followed her into the kitchen. There was a small table with wooden chairs. "It's so strange that I've never been to your home before. I don't know this part of you. And I want to."

She took two red mugs from a stand that held half a dozen and filled them with coffee from a full pot that looked freshly brewed. They sat.

"I want to come back to New York, Ash." Music to his ears. "I want you to formalize that VP position. It's wrong to base it in Dubai. I want that job and I want to be in New York."

"I want that, too. And I want us to be together. Not just as coworkers. Not as the phony couple who are now pretending to be reunited. I want to be with you for real, Annie. I love you and I want us to be together forever. I can't promise I won't make mistakes and that my past won't conspire to ruin my future. But I want to fight that fight with you. Will you do that with me? Take a chance on each other? I'll never be able to live with myself if I don't try."

"No, Ash. I need to watch after myself. No one else ever has. I can't take such dangerous odds. It's too much for me. We'll be colleagues and we'll be friends. That's all."

His heart sank at her words.

CHAPTER TWELVE

SITTING ON THE plane next to Ash, Annie hoped she'd made the right choice. He'd stayed at a Denver hotel for a few days to help her pack up her office and find a tenant to lease her house, easy as rentals were in demand. That was what was needed right now. Other decisions could be made as time went on.

"Any second thoughts?" he asked as the flight attendants prepared for takeoff. At her refusal to get back together as it were, he'd shut down into business mode, probably regretting that he'd laid his truth bare. They'd both been losers in that fight.

"It's not that Denver isn't great. But I'm so ready to try something else."

"New York isn't too bad."

She smirked as, obviously, the opportunity to live in one of the world's greatest cities was a special privilege. "Do you know what part of town you'd like to live in?"

In finalizing the plans for her return, she'd had to turn down Ash's offer to let her stay in his apartment as she had been for weeks. It wasn't going to be easy to keep things all business with him so the last thing she needed was to wake up in the morning and hear the rock 'n' roll he played in the shower and then cross paths in the kitchen, him still in a towel slung low across his hips as the angle of his pelvic bones anchored it upright. Where so many mornings she'd come face-to-face with those glorious and horrible tattoos. The ones that identified him as a warrior.

Good heavens, he'd merely asked her where she might want to live in the city of eight million people and the question had sent her mind to him in a towel. She had a long way to go in the goal of considering him as nothing more than the friend and colleague she'd insisted was all they could be. Finally, she coughed out, "Downtown, so I can be close to work."

"What features would be important to you? I'll put my leasing agent onto it."

Seeing your tattoos every morning. That would *not* be one of them.

"Good windows and high up enough for a city or river view." In other words, a mini version of his apartment.

The flight attendant served trays of snacks and offered cocktails, soft drinks and coffees.

"Orange juice."

"I'll have ginger ale." After a sip he continued, "Do you need room for your family to come visit?"

"Nope." He should have already known the answer to that question. None of her childhood issues had been resolved in adulthood. Their relationships didn't need repairing, they simply didn't exist.

"You sound sure."

She fiddled with a wedge of cheese and some strawberries.

"You don't believe change is actually possible?"

She nibbled her food. "Not fundamentally. I think people can act as though they've changed and behave as though they've changed, but then something will inevitably happen that would bring them back to their true colors." Of course, they were no longer talking about her family. They were talking about taking the chance on healing, which she knew would destroy her if it failed.

He leaned toward her with a whisper, directing the conversation to the real point,

"Even though I love you?" She had no choice but to let the words absorb into her skin. She wouldn't act on them.

He swallowed hard, dismay over his face. Putting more breaks into her heart.

He was at a loss.

She spent the next week based in a corporate hotel. She met almost daily with the VPs and department heads at EJ to truly define the new position and what her duties would be. The salary Ash proposed was considerably more than she was earning now, which would be important for the high cost of living in New York.

Everything was going great.

Except that it wasn't.

Every night when she got back to the hotel, all she did was order food in and eat it directly from the paper and plastic containers while she looked out the window at the rest of New York. She might be taking a bite of the Big Apple professionally, but what kind of personal life did she expect to have here? The same as she had in Denver which was basically not much.

It scratched at her day and night, weekday and weekend, that she'd been offered what she'd always wanted but she turned it down.

Ash. It had always been Ash. Would always be Ash. Yet she'd become so frightened by their charade and its rise and crash that she saw no option but to shield herself from any further trauma by putting up boundaries before he could.

She'd hurt herself in exact proportion to the hurt he might have bestowed on her if she'd said yes to being with him and then he'd ultimately found he couldn't go through with it. She'd been turning down his lunch plans and his dinner invitations and hiding in the metropolis. Maybe Dubai would have been better, after all.

Found an apartment I think you'll like, came a morning text. She agreed to let Ash take her to meet his leasing agent that afternoon, and the three of them went to see the rental.

"Why don't I let you two have a look around and I'll meet you downstairs in the lobby afterward?" The agent left after letting them in.

It was indeed what she'd hoped for. It had one bedroom and one bathroom, smaller than her home in Denver by many square feet, but it fit the bill for a career gal living alone. The kitchen had stainless steel appliances and the bathroom had every convenience. It did have one of those city views that made a person think everything was possible. That New York gave everyone a fresh start, a new leaf, a second look.

When she turned around from the window view to find Ash down on one knee, her eyelids fluttered uncontrollably.

"Annie, I don't think this is the right apartment for you."

She gulped. "You don't?"

"No. I think you already have two homes and that's enough."

"I don't count two," she questioned with a wobbly voice.

"You've got that beautiful property in Denver which I think we should keep. And then we have my penthouse. Don't you think that's enough for us?"

"Us?" Although, she knew. She knew before he pulled a small velvet box out of his pocket, flipped it open and held it out to her in the palm of his hand. It was an exquisite oval-cut diamond ring.

"I'm talking about your living arrangements. Me. I'm your living arrangements and I intend to be for the rest of our days on earth and then after that, too."

"What if you can't…or what if I… I couldn't live through…"

"I'll tell you what I couldn't live through and that's life without you. Marry me, Annie." He stood up and took the ring from the box to slide it on her finger. "Look how far we've already come. As long as we're together, we're limitless. We're each other's Lovieface."

He left her with no way out. How could she turn him down? He was the love of her life and something way down deep in her knew his words were the truth. *Limitless.*

Yes, they were each other's Lovieface. Also, salvation and hope and faith and joy. After all these years. They were finally ready.

* * * * *

If you enjoyed this story, check out these other great reads from Andrea Bolter

Jet-Set Escape with Her Billionaire Boss
Pretend Honeymoon with the Best Man
Adventure with a Secret Prince
Caribbean Nights with the Tycoon

All available now!

Get up to 4 Free Books!

We'll send you 2 free books from each series you try PLUS a free Mystery Gift.

FREE
Value Over
$25

Both the **Harlequin® Historical** and **Harlequin® Romance** series feature compelling novels filled with emotion and simmering romance.

YES! Please send me 2 FREE novels from the Harlequin Historical or Harlequin Romance series and my FREE Mystery Gift (gift is worth about $10 retail). After receiving them, if I don't wish to receive any more books, I can return the shipping statement marked "cancel." If I don't cancel, I will receive 5 brand-new Harlequin Historical books every month and be billed just $6.39 each in the U.S. or $7.19 each in Canada, or 4 brand-new Harlequin Romance Larger-Print books every month and be billed just $7.19 each in the U.S. or $7.99 each in Canada, a savings of 20% off the cover price. It's quite a bargain! Shipping and handling is just 50¢ per book in the U.S. and $1.25 per book in Canada.* I understand that accepting the 2 free books and gift places me under no obligation to buy anything. I can always return a shipment and cancel at any time by calling the number below. The free books and gift are mine to keep no matter what I decide.

Choose one: ☐ **Harlequin Historical**
(246/349 BPA G36Y)

☐ **Harlequin Romance Larger-Print**
(119/319 BPA G36Y)

☐ **Or Try Both!**
(246/349 & 119/319 BPA G36Z)

Name (please print)

Address _____ Apt. #

City _____ State/Province _____ Zip/Postal Code

Email: Please check this box ☐ if you would like to receive newsletters and promotional emails from Harlequin Enterprises ULC and its affiliates. You can unsubscribe anytime.

Mail to the Harlequin Reader Service:
IN U.S.A.: P.O. Box 1341, Buffalo, NY 14240-8531
IN CANADA: P.O. Box 603, Fort Erie, Ontario L2A 5X3

Want to explore our other series or interested in ebooks? Visit www.ReaderService.com or call 1-800-873-8635.

---

*Terms and prices subject to change without notice. Prices do not include sales taxes, which will be charged (if applicable) based on your state or country of residence. Canadian residents will be charged applicable taxes. Offer not valid in Quebec. This offer is limited to one order per household. Books received may not be as shown. Not valid for current subscribers to the Harlequin Historical or Harlequin Romance series. All orders subject to approval. Credit or debit balances in a customer's account(s) may be offset by any other outstanding balance owed by or to the customer. Please allow 4 to 6 weeks for delivery. Offer available while quantities last.

Your Privacy—Your information is being collected by Harlequin Enterprises ULC, operating as Harlequin Reader Service. For a complete summary of the information we collect, how we use this information and to whom it is disclosed, please visit our privacy notice located at https://corporate.harlequin.com/privacy-notice. Notice to California Residents – Under California law, you have specific rights to control and access your data. For more information on these rights and how to exercise them, visit https://corporate.harlequin.com/california-privacy. For additional information for residents of other U.S. states that provide their residents with certain rights with respect to personal data, visit https://corporate.harlequin.com/other-state-residents-privacy-rights/.

HHHRLP25